YOU PLAN YOUR SUMMER
Discover a pin-sized family living behind the walls of Grandpa's apartment. . . .
Travel to the Canadian Rockies to star in a TV movie. . . .
Escape from a giant cockroach that wants you for lunch. . . .
Search for missing gems in a mysterious old house. . . .

What happens in this book is up to the choices you make page by page.
You'll find over thirty possible endings—some funny, some scary, some surprising, some exciting. And it all starts when you decide where to spend the summer. . . .

HELP!
I'M SHRINKING!

Peggy Downing

Illustrated by Stephen D. Smith

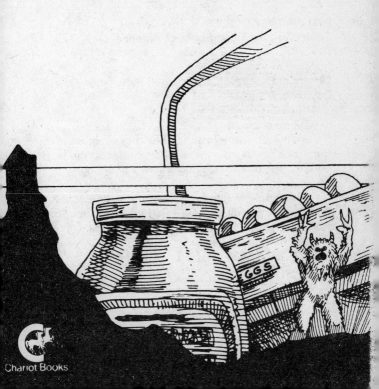

Chariot Books

For Bob

Chariot Books is an imprint of David C. Cook Publishing Co.

David C. Cook Publishing Co., Elgin, Illinois 60120
David C. Cook Publishing Co., Weston, Ontario
HELP! I'M SHRINKING!

First Printing, 1986
Printed in the United States of America
90 89 88   2 3 4 5

Library of Congress Cataloging-in-Publication Data
Downing, Peggy
  Help! I'm shrinking!
  (Making choices)
  Summary: Invited to spend summer vacation with
friends or relatives in three different places, the reader
makes decisions controlling a series of strange
adventures.
  1. Plot-your-own stories. [1. Vacations—Fiction. 2.
Adventure and adventurers—Fiction. 3. Plot-your-own
stories] I. Smith, Stephen D. ill. II. Title III. Series: Making
choices (Chariot Books)
PZ7.D75935Hf 1986   [Fic]   86-6841
ISBN 1-55513-032-1

CAUTION!

This is not a normal book! If you read it straight through, it won't make sense.

Instead, you must start on page 1 and then turn to the pages where your choices lead you. Your first choice isn't out of the ordinary: Should you spend the summer in New York City with Grandpa or in the small town of Pineville with Cousin Emily or next door with your best friends? But soon the choices take you into some unusual situations—some strange, some dangerous, and some unbelievable!

If you want to read this book, you must choose to

Turn to page 1.

One afternoon your mother says, "I want to talk to you." She looks solemn, and you try to remember what you've done or forgotten to do. She continues, "The university is sending Dad and me to Brazil to study jungle plants this summer."

You grin. "Wow. I always wanted to explore a jungle."

She shakes her head. "I'm sorry, but no children are allowed on this trip. I've already called some of our relatives. You could go to Cousin Phillip's farm."

"No way. I'd have to work too hard there."

"Would you rather visit Aunt Joyce and Uncle Pete in Pineville?"

"There's nothing to do there."

"Grandfather would be glad to see you."

"It's too hot in New York in the summer."

"You'd have fun in either New York or Pineville. Think about what you'd like to do."

Choices: You decide to go to Pineville (turn to page 5).

You agree to go to New York (turn to page 2).

You say, "I'd rather stay here and play with my friends" (turn to page 8).

Your grandfather lives in an old apartment building near Central Park. He carries your suitcase into a small bedroom as he says, "I don't know what to do. This morning my old boss called to ask if I'd come back to the chemical laboratory for a few weeks. It's exciting to think they still need me. Being retired is boring."

You answer, "Don't worry about me. I'll find plenty to do. I can explore the park and stores and museums."

"I don't know if you should wander around New York alone."

"I'm not afraid. What could happen to me in broad daylight?"

He nods. "It's worse at night, but I wish I were free to take you around. Maybe I should call my boss and tell him I can't help him."

"No, don't do that. I'll be fine."

"Some neighborhoods are dangerous. Gangs don't like strangers coming into their territory. Be careful where you go."

A shiver of fear runs up your spine.

Choices: The next day you decide to stay in the apartment when Grandfather goes to work (turn to page 3).
In the morning you go exploring (turn to page 24).

You look at Grandfather's books, but he doesn't have any fiction. You flip on the TV, but nothing looks interesting. You look out the window, wondering what you should do next. A kid about your age is looking out of a window on the south wing of the building. He waves at you, and you wave back. You're eager to find a friend, so you set out to find his apartment.

It's hard to figure out where the door is that leads to that boy's apartment. You knock on one door, but nobody answers. Then you see a sign that says, *Push Bell*. You push.

This time the door opens. It's the boy. You say, "Hi. Remember me? I waved at you from my apartment."

He smiles and says, "Hello," in a low monotone. He motions for you to come in.

A creepy sensation travels your spine. He keeps smiling and beckoning you, but he doesn't say anything.

Choices: You shake your head and leave. You don't like weirdos (turn to page 4).
You follow him (turn to page 29).

When you get back to Grandfather's apartment, you flop down on the davenport and close your eyes. You wish you were home in Seattle with your friends. It's lonely not having anyone to mess around with.

You open your eyes, wishing something exciting would happen. You blink and look again. You see five tiny people walking close to the baseboard in the kitchen. The tallest is a man who's shorter than a straight pin and almost as thin. He's dressed in tiny pants and a shirt. He picks up a crumb and hands it to the smallest figure.

"It must be a mother and father and three children," you whisper.

Choices: Grandfather will think you're crazy if you tell him you saw little people. You decide to go to the Metropolitan Museum (turn to page 103).
You decide to give the little people some food (turn to page 7).

Your folks drive you to Pineville. Uncle Pete and Aunt Joyce live close to the main part of town. They come out to greet you as you climb out of the car. Uncle Pete shakes your hand, and Aunt Joyce hugs you. She says, "Emily is busy with a chemistry experiment. She's eager to see you."

When you walk into the house, you can smell Emily's experiment. Phew! What's she trying to make—rotten eggs?

You say good-bye to your parents, who will be leaving for Brazil the next day. Mom says, "Be sure to do what Aunt Joyce says."

Dad says, "Would you like us to bring you a shrunken head from the jungle?"

"I'd rather have a monkey," you answer. Everyone laughs, and they leave. You walk outside and watch their car drive away. The lump in your throat almost chokes you.

Aunt Joyce calls, "Emily's in the basement. I'm sure she'd like to see you."

Choices: You go down to see Emily (turn to page 116).

You decline. You're not going any closer to that smell (turn to page 16).

You sit down on a patch of grass and begin eating. It might be embarrassing if Aunt Joyce asks you where you got the cherries. They sure are good—sweet and juicy.

After a while they don't taste as good. As you pop the last one in your mouth, you feel uncomfortably full. You throw the bag away and wipe your mouth.

By the time you get home, your stomach is aching, and you sneak up and lie down on your bed.

You hope you never see a cherry again.

THE END

But when you go into the kitchen, they run and disappear into the wall. You bend down and call, "Hey, come back. I'll get you some better food. How about a little piece of roast beef and a cookie?" But no one appears. Maybe the tiny people don't understand English.

You sit staring at the wall for hours. It's a long, boring day. That evening Grandfather takes you out to dinner. Afterwards you go up in the Empire State Building to see all the city lights.

When you get home, it's time for bed. During the night you wake up and head to the kitchen for a drink. The moon is shining in the window. Five tiny shadows creep across the floor. You stand perfectly still for fear of scaring them.

Suddenly two black shapes slither from a corner and head for the little people. Cockroaches! You look for a weapon. You grab a heavy cookbook, leap across the room, and swing the cookbook at the roaches, squashing one. The other escapes into the wall.

The tiny people have disappeared. You hope they got away from the cockroach that escaped your blow.

At breakfast the next morning Grandfather says, "There was a notice downstairs saying the exterminators are coming today. Cockroaches have been getting bad."

Your eyes widen in horror. "Does the stuff hurt people?"

Turn to page 80.

"You can't stay in the house alone," answers Mother.

"But I could stay next door with the Alcotts. Then I could water our lawn and stuff like that. You wouldn't have to worry about our place."

Mother looks thoughtful. "I hate to ask Sonia. She already has two kids."

"I'll ask Stone and Lia. They can talk their mother into it. They're my best friends."

"No, no," cries Mother. "Don't say anything to the twins until I've talked to their mother."

"I won't."

"I don't want Sonia to feel under any pressure. If she says it's all right, you'll have to promise me not to get into any trouble with Thurston and Thalia."

"Sure, Mom. Only don't call them Thurston and Thalia. Lia says those names sound like people from a musty old novel."

"They were named for their great-grandparents."

"All the kids call them Stone and Lia." You go outside.

Choices: You're too excited to keep quiet (turn to page 25).
You wait patiently until your mother has a chance to talk to Mrs. Alcott (turn to page 9).

Mom talks to Mrs. Alcott the next day. You wait anxiously to hear what's decided. She's smiling as she returns. "Sonia says they'll be glad to have you stay with them. But you must remember to help Mrs. Alcott and clean up after yourself."

"I will, Mom. I'm going out to see Stone and Lia."

You find them on their patio drinking lemonade. "Hi, did your mom tell you I'm going to stay with you?"

Stone nods, "Yeah, we'll have fun."

Lia says, "We're trying to figure out a way to make enough money so we can buy a computer. Got any ideas?"

You shrug. "Computers are expensive."

Stone says, "I know, but I just had a super idea. We'll start our own business—take care of houses and pets while people go on vacation."

You say slowly, "Sounds okay." But you remember that Stone's ideas often lead to trouble.

Lia adds, "We can go door to door and ask people what services they need. Almost everybody goes on vacation. We'll make a bunch of money."

Choices: You agree. "Sure, let's try it" (turn to page 14).
You answer, "I'm not going to knock on strange doors. I hate that sort of action" (turn to page 12).

You sit down by another monster. "Do we have to wear these headpieces all day?" you ask.

"Miss Balone gets cross if you mess around after she's got you costumed."

"Mine's not right. I can only see out of one eye."

"Nobody can see very well. Be glad you can breathe."

"How many monsters are there?"

"Twelve. We've been cloned. That's why we look exactly alike."

After a two-hour drive, the bus stops. You follow the others into a large snowmobile that takes you out on the Athabasca glacier. It's covered with a slippery layer of melting ice, and you walk carefully.

"Monsters, I want you to creep toward the camera waving your claws and showing your fangs," orders the director.

You feel faint as the sun beats down on you encased in your sweltering cocoon. You think of tomorrow's headline: MOVIE MONSTER DIES OF HEATSTROKE ON GLACIER.

Finally the director is satisfied, and he commands the cameraman to record the scene. All twelve of you approach the camera with menacing gestures and guttural growls. You slip on the ice and go down.

"Cut," shouts the director.

You scramble up, trying to appear inconspicuous.

"Start over," he barks.

You think, *This is not fun. And with twelve of us all alike, nobody's even going to know which one is me!*

THE END

It looks like a long, boring summer ahead. Your folks will be gone, and Stone and Lia won't be any fun if they're always working.

But that evening the phone rings and it's Aunt Marie. She's a TV star who goes by the name of Lanie LaRue. She sounds excited. "Would you like to be in a TV series?"

"You must be joking. I've never done any acting."

"This is no joke. Directors like cute kids who act natural."

"What kind of part is it?"

"You're an alien on another planet. I'm on location in the Canadian Rockies. The kid who was playing the part broke an arm. It's your big chance. Can you fly up here right away?"

You feel dizzy—as if the world's spinning too fast all of a sudden. You answer, "I'll have to ask Mom and Dad."

"Call back as soon as you decide."

You write down her number and talk to your parents. Mother says, "The decision is up to you."

You wish you could see the future so you'd know what to do. Finally you call your aunt.

Choices: You say, "Sure, I'll come" (turn to page 19).
You say, "Thanks for the offer, but I don't want to be on TV" (turn to page 82).

At dinner Grandfather asks what you've been doing all day, and you tell him about following the girl who cheated you. He says, "You could have been in real trouble. I told you to stay out of bad neighborhoods."

"I won't go there again," you promise. "But I have a funny feeling about that girl. Do you think she lives alone in that old, burned-out building?"

"Hard to tell."

"I hate her for cheating me, but I can't help feeling sorry for her."

"It's a shame there are so many homeless kids. Our church has a youth minister and some volunteers who try to help them," says Grandfather. "Maybe they'll find that girl."

"I hope somebody helps her."

"Speaking of my church—next week a Bible camp for kids your age begins. How would you like to spend a month by a cool lake?"

"Sounds great."

"I'll sign you up."

Choices: You forget about the girl who cheated you (turn to page 81).
You wish you could help the girl who lives in that half-burned building (turn to page 95).

By the time your folks leave, Lia has drawn a map of the neighborhood, and you all agree to canvass certain blocks. The twins have worked out a price list, starting with basic house care which includes picking up mail and watering. It costs more for pet care, mowing, and other garden work.

You look over the list. "Guess you've thought of everything."

In the afternoon you walk to the three blocks near the woods. No one is home in the first four houses. At the next house the lady says, "The Grubers watch our place and we watch the Grubers'."

You try the house on the other side of Grubers. A man growls, "Never buy anything from door-to-door salesmen. Why can't you leave me alone so I can sleep? I work nights."

"Sorry." You back off down the stairs. What a grouch. You go into the woods and sit on a fallen log.

When you return to the Alcotts, Stone meets you. "How many did you get?"

"Most of the people weren't home or they watch each other's houses."

"Didn't you get anyone? I got four people and Lia got two, and she's still working. I'll give you another block."

Choices: You go out again (turn to page 76).
You say, "I've done enough for today" (turn to page 142).

You walk around the outside of the house thinking what a long summer it's going to be.

You notice an old house sitting on top of the hill, and you trudge up the road toward it. It's three stories high and narrow. It looks a little tilted as if it's too old to withstand the winter winds. The brown paint's peeling, and a dead tree in the front yard looks as forlorn as the house.

It would make a good Halloween haunted house. You stop halfway up the hill. Even though the June sun is baking your back, you shiver. You don't want to go any closer. You turn back as you hear Aunt Joyce calling you to supper.

Aunt Joyce serves a picnic supper in the backyard—which is a good thing considering how the house smells. Emily drones on about chemistry experiments while you think how boring the summer is going to be.

Turn to page 18.

You say, "Who lives in that house on the hill?"

Aunt Joyce answers, "That's Mr. Norman's house, but he died a month ago. His daughter Susan Fellar inherited the house and all his gems."

"Gems?" you echo.

"Mr. Norman was a jeweler," explains Uncle Pete. "He collected big stones—sapphires, diamonds, emeralds, rubies. They say his collection was worth half a million."

Emily inserts, "The gems won't do Mrs. Fellar any good if she can't find them."

You ears prick up. "What happened to the gems?"

"No one knows," sighs Aunt Joyce. "Susan's been searching that house from top to bottom. No gems."

Uncle Pete adds, "Some think Mr. Norman's hired man took them, but nobody can prove anything. Susan's a widow, and she needs the money from the gems. She broke her leg so she's in the hospital right now. But she'll be coming back any day."

When you finish eating, Emily says, "Want to help me take out my telescope?"

Choices: You answer, "Not now. I'm going exploring" (turn to page 45).

You shrug and say, "Okay" (turn to page 58).

Now that you've made your decision, you feel excited. You run next door to tell Stone and Lia about trying for a TV part. Stone says, "Let's have a celebration."

"I don't have much time. I leave for Canada tomorrow."

But Lia invites a bunch of friends for a quick party. You drink lemonade and munch cookies on the patio. One of your best friends exclaims, "Are you really going to be on TV?"

Choices: You brag about being a star (turn to page 36).
You try to play down your importance (turn to page 131).

"I'm asking people if they want someone to watch their houses while they're on vacation."

"Can't make any money that way."

"I can too. I just got a customer."

"Who would want a kid watching his house?"

"Mrs. Stark would."

"Oh, yeah? Where are the Starks going?"

"They're driving to Yellowstone next week."

"Nice park." Drag goes back to working on his car.

You feel uneasy. Maybe you shouldn't have told Drag the Starks were going to be gone. It just sort of slipped out.

When you get back to Alcotts, Stone says, "We got nine places altogether. How many did you get?"

"Only one, but there's a cat to take of so we'll get extra money."

Stone grumbles, "You're not much of a salesman."

Lia says, "I'll work out a schedule."

Turn to page 22.

The hole is a crack in the wood, just big enough for you, but too small for the cockroach. You slip through the crack, entering a small room where the family of little people are sitting on the floor eating bits of bread.

They stare at you with fearful eyes. You say, "I've come to warn you. The exterminators are coming this morning to kill the cockroaches. Please come with me, or you'll be killed, too."

"Who are you?" demands the father.

"There's no time to explain. Come, we have to get out of the building."

"Halls are thick with cockroaches," points out the mother. "No way we can get out without being eaten. Used to be lots of us on the third floor. After the cockroaches moved up here, people disappeared. I always . . ."

You interrupt. "Hurry. We'll go through the apartment to the fire escape."

"The giants are out there," cries the oldest boy.

You answer, "The giants won't eat you. Come on. We can keep hidden from them." You lead the way out through the crack. A stinging smell makes you cough. "Hurry, hurry!" You look at your watch. Five after nine.

The smallest child faints. "It may be too late," says the father as he picks up the child.

Turn to page 46.

After the Starks leave, you go to their house twice a day to pick up papers and mail and to feed Precious. She eats expensive, fishy-smelling cat food. At first Precious hides when you come in the kitchen. But when she realizes you're the one feeding her, she rubs against you and purrs loudly.

On the third day when you go in the house, you gasp. Drawers have been emptied from the dining room buffet. The large TV set is missing. All the books in the bookcase have been dumped on the floor. Someone has searched the house looking for valuables. A cold hard lump settles in your stomach.

You look for Precious, but you can't find her. She must be hiding. The burglars must have scared her. What if she ran away? You try not to think of the terrible possibilities.

You call the police. A couple of detectives come and ask you questions. They take fingerprints, but they don't say much.

"Can you get the stuff back?" you ask.

"Not much chance. You can't even give us a list of what's missing. When the resident returns, the trail's going to be cold. Keep your eyes open and let us know if you see anything suspicious." They leave.

You wonder if you should have told them about Drag, but you don't have any proof—only your strong suspicions.

You go back to tell Stone what happened.

Choices: You tell him about Drag (turn to page 47).

You don't mention Drag (turn to page 128).

You walk down a street with many stores. Your folks gave you fifty dollars for spending money, and it feels good to have that much in the wallet in your pocket. You don't expect to spend much; mainly you're looking for postcards to send to your friends.

You walk along the sidewalk looking in the windows of the shops. A slim girl a little taller than you catches up with you. "Hey, want to earn fifty dollars?" She flips her long black hair back with her hand.

"Doing what?"

"Taking part in a survey for a TV company."

You feel excited. "Yeah, sure, I'll do that."

"All you have to do is pay me ten dollars, and I'll give you a ticket to the TV studio."

You look at her suspiciously. She's wearing jeans and a pink T-shirt. You wonder why they picked her to sell tickets. You ask, "When do I get my fifty dollars?"

"After you fill out some stuff. It's easy money."

Choices: You don't trust her, so you say, "No, thanks. It's not my style" (turn to page 35).

You pull ten dollars from your wallet and hand it to her (turn to page 28).

You rush out to find the twins. They're shooting baskets at a hoop in front of their garage. You grab the ball and say, "Got some news."

"What?" asks Stone.

"My folks are going to Brazil, but they can't take me. Think I can stay at your house?"

Lia nods. "Sure, we've got an extra room."

"Will your mom care?"

"We can talk her into it," says Stone.

You toss the ball into the basket and the game resumes.

The next day Mom asks, "Why did you disobey me?"

"Huh?"

"I talked to Sonia this morning. She says you can stay with them, but I feel the twins have been putting a lot of pressure on her. I asked you not to say anything."

You squirm. "I guess I let it slip out."

"You need to obey even when you think you know best. I've just talked to Cousin Phillip, and he says they'd love to have you visit the farm."

"Mom! I'll spend all summer picking strawberries, raspberries, cucumbers—I'll have to get up at dawn."

But you can tell by Mom's expression that it's all settled. Your big mouth led you to a sentence of hard labor.

THE END

Bruce begins to show you signals for whole words. It's going to take a long time to learn to talk fast with your hands. During the next few weeks he takes you to see the sights of New York—like the Statue of Liberty and Bronx Zoo. He knows the subway and bus routes, and you practice signing as you travel.

One morning Bruce signs from his window, "Come over."

You sign back, "I'll be there."

Then Bruce signs, "HELP! J-O-E-Y!" He points to the windowsill.

Joey is two and lives in the next apartment. You rush out the door. Joey's mother is down the hall talking to a neighbor. The door's open, and you hurry inside.

Joey's straddling the windowsill. "Horsey," he says. You gulp as you think of the hard cement courtyard three floors down.

Turn to page 34.

She gives you the ticket and tells you how to get to the television building. You walk toward it, thinking how you'll spend your fifty dollars—really only forty because the ticket cost you ten.

A lot of people are standing in the lobby. A man checks your ticket and tells you to wait with the others.

A little later you're led into a room with theater-type seats. A woman explains that you'll see a pilot for a possible new TV show.

The film is about a teenage boy who invents a wrist computer that prints other people's thoughts on its small screen. The first episode shows him revealing the identity of an embezzler in his father's bank. As you watch, you have two buttons to press—one when you like the part you're watching and the other when you don't like it.

You think the computer idea is clever, but the rest of the plot is silly. You write this on the questionnaire you fill out.

The woman thanks you for your cooperation, and people begin to file out. Nobody hands you any payment.

Choices: You complain (turn to page 41).
You realize that you've been duped and go back to the apartment (turn to page 4).

He shows you a computer in the den. He quickly types. "I'm Bruce. I can't hear. Please type what you said."

You read his message on the screen. You can't type fast the way he does, but you pick out the answer. "I'm the one who waved."

He types, "Want to learn sign language so we can talk better?"

"Is it hard?"

"At first, but you'll soon get the hang of it. I'm learning to lip-read and talk, but signing is the easiest for me."

You type, "I have lots of time. Go ahead. Teach me."

First he shows you how to form the alphabet with your hands. It takes a while to learn, but you finally learn all the letters.

You slowly sign, "T-A-K-E-S T-O-O L-O-N-G."

Bruce types, "All the common words have their own sign. You don't have to spell much."

You frown and type, "You mean I have a lot more to learn?"

Bruce nods.

Choices: You type, "This is too hard. I have to go. Bye" (turn to page 4).
You stay (turn to page 26).

You read the first script in the regular series. When you see Aunt Marie at dinner you say, "I don't like that script. In the pilot I played a good character, but here Sylmar is lying, cheating, and hurting other people."

Aunt Marie shrugs. "Oh, the kids will still like you."

"But I don't want them to like me if I lie and cheat."

"It's just a story."

You explain, "In Sunday school last year we studied the Ten Commandments. We listed shows where characters broke God's commandments. We put down our reactions—like laughing, feeling sad, feeling angry, or wanting the character to succeed. Then we talked about it, and we decided when the hero broke a commandment it was worse than when the villain did."

Turn to page 42.

Your feet hurt and your stomach growls. Finally you find a service station and call your aunt.

She says, "We've been so worried. When the Dilmers came back to say you were lost, several of the men went to search for you."

"Hey, if they were looking for me, how come nobody was in the parking lot when I got there?"

"I don't know. You tell me exactly where you are, and I'll send someone after you."

Turn to page 135.

You tell your friends about the dollar swimming pool. The next day you have a blast. You take in fifteen dollars, but the best part is having so much fun.

Word gets around, and on the second day sixty kids show up with their dollars. You collect the money, and you whisper to Stone, "I hope we don't have a riot when the kids see how crowded the pool is."

You walk around the pool hoping no one gets hurt in the wiggling mass of humanity.

A big kid climbs on the diving board. "Get out of my way," he shouts.

"Too crowded for diving," you yell.

"Says who?" He dives in, smashing into another guy. They start fighting.

Stone hollers, "Stop fighting or I'll close the pool."

"You and who else?" demands a muscular fellow.

A red-haired girl shrieks, "I can't find my sister!"

Another girl climbs out of the pool. "Make those tough kids go home."

You swallow and look at Stone. The two fighters climb out of the pool and resume their fighting using the Fullers' aluminum chairs as weapons. "Stop, stop," yells Stone.

"I think my sister drowned!" screams the redhead.

"Ahhhh, there's a body down here!" cries a small boy.

Choices: **You run off. Somebody's going to get in trouble, but it's not going to be you (turn to page 50).**

You try to help (turn to page 40).

You try not to excite him. You walk closer until you can grab him.

His mother returns and exclaims, "What's going on?"

"Joey was on the windowsill. He could have fallen."

She takes him from you. "No, no climb on windowsill." She looks at you suspiciously. "How'd you know he was on the sill?"

You tell her about Bruce and how you're learning signing.

She squeezes Joey. "You kids may have saved Joey's life. I'll never leave that window open again. Thank you, and tell your friend thanks."

You hurry down to Bruce's apartment to tell him all is well.

THE END

You walk toward Central Park. As you walk along the sidewalk, you pass an old lady moving slowly. You spin around as you hear a cry. The woman has fallen. You run back. "Can I help you up?"

"No, no. I think my arm is broken. I felt something snap. Oh, what am I going to do now? Where's my purse? Did someone take it?"

You pick up the shabby black purse. "It's right here." You hang onto it as a couple of guys saunter by.

Then an older man stops. "What happened?"

"Broke my arm," she answers. "Oh, it hurts."

"I'll call an ambulance," he offers.

"I'll stay with her until the ambulance comes," you say. A crowd gathers. You hang onto the purse tightly.

Finally the ambulance arrives. You hand the woman her purse as they lift her on the stretcher. She says to you, "Thanks. Oh, please, could you tell Mrs. Folisky what happened. I'm supposed to baby-sit for her." She points to a building across the street. "She lives in apartment 907."

Her stretcher is lifted into the back of the ambulance before you can answer.

Choices: You look up Mrs. Folisky (turn to page 53).

You go on to a museum (turn to page 103).

You answer, "My aunt's a star, and she says I'm right for this part."

"Some kids have all the luck," says Stone.

It feels great to have all the kids staring at you like you're somebody famous. You announce, "I won't forget my friends even when I'm a star. Come out to Hollywood to visit me. I'll introduce you to some of the big stars. You can swim in my pool."

"I thought you were going to Canada," says Stone.

"We're filming there on location, but we'll do a lot of scenes at the studio in Hollywood."

"I wish I were going," sighs Lia.

"If anybody wants my autograph now before I get too busy, just let me know." You start to reach for another glass of lemonade, but someone pours it for you. Lia gets some paper, and you begin signing your name. "Might as well get in practice," you say.

The next day you land at the airport in Calgary. "Hi, Aunt Marie," you shout.

She frowns. "Please call me Miss LaRue. I don't want people to think I'm pushing a relative."

You climb in your aunt's car and head west toward Banff. The Rocky Mountains stand in sharp contrast to the flat plains. When you come to the mountains, the road winds upward.

Your aunt has a suite of rooms in a Banff hotel. She shows you your bedroom. "Tomorrow morning will be the auditions." She hands you a script to study.

You try to swallow the fuzzy lump in your throat.

That evening you and your aunt join the other actors and actresses for dinner in the dining room. A kid named Chris Dilmer sits beside you. "I hear you're trying out for the part of Sylmar, too. What shows have you been in?"

You pretend you don't hear. "Pass the butter."

"Never heard of that one. What drama schools you been to?"

"Some things you don't learn in school."

"Why don't you answer my questions? I know why. You've never been in a show and you've never been in drama school. You don't have a chance."

Choices: You're determined to beat that conceited Chris (turn to page 39).

You agree with Chris that you don't have a chance (turn to page 62).

You look behind **you**. The cockroach is still coming. Your side **aches** and you're panting.

As you round a corner, two more roaches rush **toward** you. You're trapped. Teeth sink into your leg. HELP! They're **fighting** over you. Pain signals flash to your **brain**. There's no **way** to escape.

You feel dizzy, but you gulp air, fighting the sick feeling. You hit the hard-shelled roaches with your tiny fists.

Turn to page 51.

You don't sleep much that night, and by the next morning your stomach feels as if sea gulls are flapping their wings there.

Aunt Marie says, "Breathe deeply. Don't look as if you're going to your execution."

"I think I've changed my mind."

"Everybody gets nervous before an audition. Once you start reading everything will be fine. Just concentrate on Sylmar. You are Sylmar. You're not your self. You're a slave on the planet Eyesig."

Your audition is at nine. By the time you begin, your voice sounds hoarse.

The director shouts, "Start again."

But it's even worse the next time. This time he doesn't stop you. You try to be Sylmar, but other thoughts keep flashing in your mind. "That conceited Chris will get the part. Aunt Marie will be disappointed. What will I tell my friends?"

When you finish reading, the director says, "You're too uptight. If you want to work on camera, you'll have to relax. Get some experience and try again in a few years."

The sea gulls have stopped flapping. Instead you feel a heavy stone in your stomach.

Choices: **You want to go home (turn to page 44).**
You decide to stick around to watch the filming (turn to page 75).

You jump in near the boy who gave the alarm. Your heart pounds as you dive under the water and pull up the small girl. "Get out of the way," you gasp as you surface.

A boy helps you lift her from the pool. You take a big gulp of air and put your mouth over hers, blowing air into her lungs. You try to concentrate on what you learned in your life-saving class. But this time it's for real, and your heart's beating like a jackhammer. Finally you feel the girl gasp. She's breathing again.

A few minutes later the police arrive with the Fullers' son Greg. You learn later that he came to check on his parents' house, heard the commotion, and called for help.

The police quickly give the girl oxygen, separate the fighters, and clear the pool.

Stone tries to explain to Greg Fuller, "We're taking care of your parents' place. We let some friends swim, but then some tough guys came and ruined everything."

You tell Greg, "We're sorry about the damage." You give him all the money you collected. "If this isn't enough to pay for new chairs, we'll give you more."

The police rush the girl to the hospital. That evening you hear on the news that she's fine. You'll never forget how hard you tried to get that small body to breath again. "Thank you, Lord," you whisper.

THE END

You walk back into the room, squirming among the people who are leaving. You finally reach the woman in charge. "I was told I'd get fifty dollars for taking part in this survey."

"Who told you that?" she asks.

"The girl who sold me the ticket."

"The tickets are free. If anyone sold you one, she wasn't working for us. I'm sorry, but someone took advantage of you."

You feel your blood boiling, but there's no use getting mad at the woman. It wasn't her fault. You leave.

Choices: **You decide to look for the girl who sold you the ticket (turn to page 52). You try to forget the whole thing and go back to the apartment (turn to page 4).**

Aunt Marie leans back in her chair. "TV shows don't have anything to do with real life."

"Our class feels they influence the way kids think. Badness and goodness get all confused. I don't want to play Sylmar—not the way the role is now."

"But we need you. You can be a good influence by showing your Christian faith in the way you live off screen."

Choices: You agree to stay on as Sylmar (turn to page 146).
You say, "I wouldn't feel right about being Sylmar now" (turn to page 127).

"Who are you?" snarls Mr. Belden.

"I was just walking by."

"I can use some help. Want a job?"

"Doing what?"

"I'll show you." He's still gripping your arm and you're scared. He snaps off the light and points to a stairway. You start down the stairs, with only the dim light of Mr. Belden's flashlight to guide you.

The basement is musty and dusty. One wall has shelves full of canned goods. "Looks like a grocery store," you mutter.

"Old Man Norman was eccentric—liked to have lots of food on hand." Mr. Belden points to a hole in a far corner. "Go down." A ladder leads to a dirt root cellar below the cement basement.

You look at the dark hole and shudder. "Don't make me go down there."

"Quit sniveling. I've been digging but I'm tired. You can dig for a while. Good exercise."

You climb down the ladder and pick up the shovel. Mr. Belden shines his flashlight on you. "Get busy, kid."

The air is damp and moldy smelling. There's a hole in the middle of the dirt floor, and you begin to dig in the hard-packed earth. You have to think of a way to escape.

Choices: You try to reason with Mr. Belden (turn to page 117).

You try to scare Mr. Belden (turn to page 108).

You take an airporter from Banff to the Calgary airport. As you ride home on the jet, you think how surprised Stone and Lia will be to learn you're going to stay with them after all.

But then you think, *What'll I tell my friends? I shouldn't have bragged about being a star. I'll tell them I didn't like the part, so I'm waiting for a better role—or maybe I should say the director liked my acting, but I didn't look right for an alien.*

You look out at the bright, billowy clouds below you. "Hey," you say to yourself, "how about the truth?" You were scared out of your skull, and you blew your audition. Your friends will understand.

"Actually they'll probably like me better now that I'm back to being an ordinary kid instead of bragging about being a star."

THE END

You walk toward town. You go into a discount store and start playing a video game. The boy at the next game asks, "You new in town?"

"I'm visiting the Coopers."

"You a brain, too?"

"Not like Emily."

He says, "Interested in making some money?"

"Depends on what I have to do."

"Pick cherries. We can make good money. My name's Jeff. I live in the yellow house at the end of Main Street. Meet me there tomorrow at nine."

Choices: You say, "I'll be there" (turn to page 134).

You answer, "Count me out. It's too hot for hard labor." You go back to look through Emily's telescope (turn to page 58).

"No, we can make it." You slip through the hole into the apartment, followed by the tiny family. But the smell is there, too, and everyone is coughing.

"Mommy, I feel sick," cries the middle girl.

You look frantically around. Where can you go? Crossing the living room through the thick, trackless rug will take time. You feel weak, and every step is a great effort.

You feel very strange. Then you realize what's happening. You're growing big again. A sudden dizziness forces you to lie down. You close your eyes.

When you open them, you find you've grown back to your normal size. As you look around, you see the tiny people are lying still.

You grab a cake pan and put each person in it. Then you rush out to the fire escape at the end of the hall. You watch the still forms, hoping the fresh air will revive them. Finally the father stirs. You see terror in his eyes as he looks up into your huge eyes.

"I'm a friend," you say. He puts his hands over his ears to shut out the loud noise of your voice. He looks around at his still family.

You put the pan down on the fire escape.

Choices: **You go back in the apartment (turn to page 48).**

You sit in a corner of the fire escape (turn to page 68).

You say, "Stone, I think it might have been Drag."

"He got in a lot of trouble at school, but what makes you think he'd rob somebody?"

You gulp. "I sort of let it slip that the Starks were going on vacation. As soon as I said it, I knew I shouldn't have, but—there was no way to unsay my words."

"You could ruin our whole operation if the word gets out that we blab about who's going to be gone."

"I won't ever do it again. We've got to get the stuff back."

"How are we going to do that?"

"I wonder if we could get in Drag's house. I'd know that TV set if I saw it again."

"Hey, we don't want to land in jail. Maybe we can just look in the windows."

Choices: You agree to looking in windows (turn to page 72).

You tell Stone it's your problem, and you're going to solve it yourself (turn to page 94).

You think, *this sure has been a crazy morning.* You feel hungry so you look in the cupboard for the package of chocolate chip cookies. You pour yourself some milk.

When you finish your midmorning snack, you go back to the fire escape. A big orange cat is reaching his clawed paw into the pan of little people.

"No, no," you scream.

The cat darts away, and you look down to see if the people are hurt. One child is missing!"

Choices: You chase the cat (turn to page 113).
You bring the rest of the family into the safety of the apartment (turn to page 125).

You run home. You aren't going to stay there with guys fighting and kids screaming about bodies. The whole mess was Stone's idea. It wasn't your fault it turned into a disaster. You turn on the sprinklers in the backyard.

Near dinnertime you go back to Alcotts. Stone says, "A fine friend you turned out to be. What happened to you?"

"I had to water our lawn."

Stone shakes his head. "Everything fell apart! Greg Fuller came to check on his folks' place, and when he saw the riot, he called the police. We tried to explain that we were taking care of the house. For a while I thought they were going to take us to jail."

Lia says, "That's not the worst. A little girl almost drowned. She's in the hospital in critical condition. They hope she'll live, but they're not sure."

Stone adds, "Her folks are going to sue Fullers, our folks, and your folks."

"My folks?" you gulp.

"Sure," explains Stone. "You're part of the house-watching business."

You don't feel hungry anymore. You're thinking of what your parents will say when they come home to find a lawsuit facing them. But even worse is the thought that maybe you could have helped that girl if you hadn't panicked.

THE END

The roaches back off, but not because of your fists. You're starting to grow! The strange-tasting liquid must be wearing off. You're glad, but there's not much room between the boards. Ouch.

You cry, "HELP! THE WALL IS SQUASHING ME!" You push against the rough boards, but nothing gives. You're getting bigger, but the wall acts like a torture device—squeezing your body. Your nerves scream in pain. You fight for breath.

You again push with all your might against the wall. The boards break, and you go crashing into an apartment bedroom.

A woman in bed screams.

Choices: You leave fast (turn to page 88).
You try to explain what happened (turn to page 148).

You walk back to the street where the girl sold you the ticket. You see lots of people, but not her. With all the people in New York, there's not much chance you'll find her. Even if you did, what would you do? Maybe if you threatened to call a cop, she'd give you your ten dollars back.

You keep looking at faces. She had a pretty face except for a large mole under her right eye.

You walk into a drugstore to buy postcards, but they don't have any you like. When you come out, you see the girl hurrying by. You look for a policeman, but none are around. Maybe the best idea is to find out where she lives. If you knew her address, you could threaten to send the police after her.

You keep trailing her the way spies do on TV. She heads down the stairway of a subway entrance.

Choices: You follow her (turn to page 83).
You give up. It wouldn't be smart to get on a subway when you don't even know where it's going (turn to page 35).

You run across the street to the apartment building. The doorman lets you in, and you find Mrs. Folisky's apartment on the ninth floor.

Mrs. Folisky frowns as she opens the door. "I thought you were Mrs. Campbell, the sitter."

You explain what happened to her baby-sitter.

She cries, "What'll I do? I have an important job interview in half an hour." Then she looks at you and pleads, "Could you watch Jerome? I'll pay well and only be gone a couple of hours."

"I guess I can," you answer. You follow her inside.

"Here's Jerome. He's two and a half."

Jerome zooms his tricycle straight at you.

His mother grabs him off the trike. "Jerome, darling, we never ride our trike in the apartment, remember."

She kisses him and leaves. You say, "Hi, Jerome."

"Wanta ride trike."

"Not in the apartment," you remind him.

"In hall," he says.

You don't know what the rules are about that. You open the door and peek out. The hall is deserted. "Okay," you agree.

Jerome roars out to the carpeted hall.

"Don't make so much noise," you say.

Turn to page 64.

You go back to dry ground and find a grassy spot by the lake. The sun warms your back, and you feel sleepy.

Suddenly a green scaly head on a long neck pops up near the shore. Big, yellow eyes stare at you. You stare back, too petrified to move.

He splashes toward you, and you see the rest of his body. He's huge—like a dinosaur. Your heart's pounding, and you can't get enough air. He opens his mouth, baring large, pointed teeth. You order your legs to run, but they keep shaking like the rest of you.

But instead of eating you, he says in a growlly voice, "Hey, where am I?"

You gasp, "Washington State—near Pineville."

"Great warty dragons! I knew I got my directions mixed. I'm heading for Lake Tahoe."

"Are you from Scotland? Are you the Loch Ness Monster?"

"No, no, not me. That's my uncle. He's a big show-off. The rest of us keep out of sight—most of the time, that is."

THE END

"Emily, wake up quick."

"Huh? Hey, it's still dark." She pulls her blanket over her head.

You pull it off. "Emily, Mr. Belden is chopping up the Norman house. Please, help!"

"What can I do?"

"Get one of your burglar bombs. The smell will drive him away."

"I don't want to tangle with Mr. Belden."

"But he's ruining Mrs. Fellar's house. Come on. If we're careful, he won't see us."

Emily puts a coat over her pajamas and goes to her laboratory to get her burglar bomb.

You both run up the hill and then sneak up to the house. Your heart is pounding as you creep up the stairs. "I'm scared," whispers Emily.

"Shhh," you warn. You push the front door open, and Emily tosses her stink bomb in. You can smell it working before you get off the porch.

You hide with Emily behind a bush.

Mr. Belden runs out and drives away.

Choices: You say, "Come on, Emily. I know where the gems are" (turn to page 147).

You say, "Let's go home—away from that terrible smell" (turn to page 110).

The next day Lia assigns you the Elliotts' house. It's in back of your house. They have a big, shaggy dog named Zacchaeus. He's overly friendly and likes to lick faces with his rough, slobbery tongue.

On Monday all seven Elliotts pile into their station wagon and leave for their vacation. As soon as Zacchaeus realizes he's been left behind, he starts to howl. You pet him and snap on his leash to take him for a walk.

When you open the gate, he runs off in the direction he saw the station wagon go. You soon realize he's taking you for a run instead of you taking him for a walk.

"Stop, Zacchaeus. STOP!" you gasp.

Choices: You look for help (turn to page 85).
You keep running (turn to page 150).

When it starts to get dark, you help Emily carry out her telescope—the heavy stand, the four-foot tube with the reflector mirror, and the box of eyepieces. After she gets everything together, Emily tells you to look in the eyepiece. You squint and see a fuzzy star. "What is it?"

"The Andromeda galaxy. It has millions of stars like our Milky Way."

"Oh, wow, that's fantastic."

As she's adjusting the scope, you look at the Norman house. You cry, "Emily, quick let me use your telescope. Somebody's in the basement of the Norman house. Maybe they're looking for the gems!"

Emily points her telescope toward the house. "I don't see anyone."

"Let me look." You hold your eye against the eyepiece. You try to move the scope, but then you lose the window.

"I'll adjust it," says Emily. She moves the scope and exclaims, "That's Mr. Belden. He used to be Mr. Norman's hired hand. Can't see his face, but I recognize his red hair."

"He must be looking for the gems. We've got to stop him," you cry.

"Don't be an idiot. How can we do that?"

"We could call the sheriff."

"Maybe Susan Fellar asked him to watch the place. We don't know he's doing anything wrong. Besides he's mean, and I don't want him mad at me."

Choices: You go back to your room (turn to page 152).

You sneak over to the house (turn to page 74).

You dial the sheriff's number and explain what happened. In a few minutes you hear sirens. You run back up the hill.

Mr. Belden runs out of the house and heads for his car. As he's opening his door, the sheriff's car stops behind him.

"Hands up," yells the sheriff.

His deputy starts asking questions. "You can't prove nothing," Mr. Belden mutters.

You walk up and tell what you saw. Mr. Belden glares at you. The sheriff orders you all inside. You see that Mr. Belden has chopped holes in the walls and floor of the living room.

The sheriff says, "Good thing you called us before he ruined the whole house." He puts handcuffs on Mr. Belden.

When you come out, you see your aunt, uncle, and Emily. A reporter snaps a picture of you, Mr. Belden, and the sheriff.

When the paper comes out, the headline reads, KID SAVES NORMAN HOUSE. Around Pineville, you're famous!

THE END

You climb up a sturdy cherry tree and begin filling a large plastic sack Jeff gave you. The cherries are sweet, and you pop the biggest ones in your mouth, spitting out the seeds. When your sack's full, you climb down and put it on Jeff's wagon.

You grab another sack and climb back up the same tree.

Jeff, in a tree near you, calls, "Oh, oh, I hear Old Man Morton's dogs. We better run."

Choices: You agree with Jeff (turn to page 78).
You stay in the tree (turn to page 115).

When you wake up the morning of the audition, you think, "After today I can go home. It was dumb to think I could be a star." You don't feel nervous, because you know there's no way they're going to pick you.

You read for the director, and he waves his arms as if he's excited. You hope he's not mad at Aunt Marie for bringing you. He tells you to read another page. Finally he says, "You have a great natural talent. It's rare to find anyone like you."

You stare at him. "You mean, I get the part?"

"Of course. You're just what I want for Sylmar."

You look for Aunt Marie to tell her the news, but you can't find her.

You run into a hairy monster in the hotel lobby. You recognize Chris Dilmer's voice coming from a gruesome silver-green headpiece. "Congratulations. I hear you're going to be Sylmar."

"News travels fast around here."

"Oh, we're just one happy family. We compete for parts, but once the decision is made, we work to make a great film." Chris pulls off the headpiece. "I'm going to be a snow monster, and that will be fun. Want to go on a hike?"

Choices: You say, "No, I have to study the script" (turn to page 98).

You agree. "Sounds great" (turn to page 138).

You're too excited to sleep that night. You keep thinking about what you'll do with the gems. You'll sell them to buy stuff like a ten-speed bike, a TV with a video-cassette recorder, and a computer to do your schoolwork.

Part of you worries that Mr. Belden won't keep his promise. But if he doesn't, you'll threaten to tell what you know. He'll have to give you your share of the gems to keep you quiet.

Turn to page 118.

"Motor. Trike has motor." He does a fair imitation of a large truck.

You hear the phone ringing, and you run to answer it. "No, Mrs. Folisky isn't home."

You step back to the hall. Jerome has disappeared. A stone of fear settles in your stomach. "Jerome," you call. "Where are you?" You run down the hall looking for him. You knock on doors. No one answers. Finally a lady in a pink robe opens her door a crack. You ask if she's seen Jerome.

She sounds annoyed. "Kids aren't supposed to live in this building. It's only because that couple has been here so long that they're allowed to stay." She closes her door.

The elevator door opens, and you feel another queasy sensation. You ride downstairs. The doorman assures you that no two-year-old on a trike rode past him.

He must still be in the building, but where? You run up the stairs looking up and down the halls, listening for the roar of the trike. You push the thought of kidnapping from your mind.

No one is on the first three floors. You decide it would be easier to run downstairs, so you take the elevator to the top. You get off in a small hallway and see a door marked *roof garden.*

You open the door and see Jerome zooming around between the potted plants. How wonderful a roaring trike sounds!

THE END

That night you tell Grandfather you want to go home. He says, "You can't go home when your folks aren't there."

"I can stay with the people next door."

"Are you sure?"

"Yeah, I'm sure. My best friends live there— Stone and Lia."

Grandfather rubs his chin. "I'd better call and make sure." Grandfather calls the Alcotts and then makes your plane reservation.

You're happy to be going home. You can't afford to stay in New York at almost fifty dollars a day.

THE END

You follow the girl to a building which has been partly destroyed by a fire. The girl slips through the glassless window into the basement.

You peer into the darkness. You holler, "Is this where you live?"

"What's it to you?" she snaps.

"If you give me my ten dollars back, I won't sic the cops on you."

"You can't prove nothing. Get going or you'll wish you had."

You see a couple of tough-looking guys watching from across the street. You decide to leave quick-like. By the time you get out of the neighborhood, you're out of breath and sweating like a defrosting turkey.

Choices: **You decide to tell Grandfather about your adventures (turn to page 13).**
You decide not to tell Grandfather (turn to page 69).

You guard the pan, hoping they won't notice you and become frightened.

The mother comes to next, and she bustles around her children, trying to revive them.

The father looks down from the pan. The fire escape is made of metal slats, and the tiny people could easily fall between them. You figure the father is worried about how they're going to get back to their safe hiding place.

The children all come to. You see them talking to one another, but their voices are so soft your ears can't hear any sound.

Later you slip back into the apartment. You can't smell the gas anymore. You grab a piece of bread to take to them. You sprinkle some crumbs on the pan, but the little people look up at you with fear. Finally they eat some of the bread.

After they've eaten, you take them back to the apartment.

Choices: You lift the people out of their pan so they can return to their hidden room (turn to page 70).

You put the pan in the cupboard and close the door. You hope they'll take a nap while you prepare a surprise (turn to page 77).

Grandfather asks, "You have a good day?"

"It was okay." You don't want to worry him, so you don't tell him what you did.

"I had a great day. Sure is good to be working again. Funny thing about people. We don't quite know what we want. For forty years I've looked forward to retiring so I could sleep as long as I want and do anything I felt like. But after about a month that got monotonous. People aren't happy unless they're accomplishing something."

"Is that why summer vacation gets boring sometimes?"

"Exactly. But it doesn't have to be boring. You should be writing down what you're learning this summer. New York is full of interesting places and people to study."

That's for sure! You could write a story about today's adventure—a horror story.

THE END

After the little people have gone, you put the pan away. You've had an exciting adventure. You think back, trying to remember how it felt to be small. It seems unreal, almost like a dream, but it really happened.

But no one's going to believe it. What good is an adventure you can't talk about?

THE END

You sink into the nearest empty seat on the bus. You're glad the bus starts right away, before Drag can follow you.

You get off at the local business district and head for the police station. You tell the receptionist, "I have evidence about a robbery."

You wait until a detective can talk to you. It's one of the men who came out to the Stark house. He listens to your tape twice. "We'll get a search warrant and go out to Drag's house right away. Thanks for your help."

You go back to the Alcotts and tell Stone and Lia what happened. In the evening a reporter comes out to take your picture. He wants to write about the clever way you collected evidence. The police have reported they recovered stolen goods from a large number of robberies in Drag's shed.

"Wow," says Stone, "this is going to be great publicity for our business."

You groan. You're getting tired of house and cat sitting.

THE END

That evening when dusk comes, you, Stone, and Lia walk over to Drag's house. You quietly sneak around the house. "All the drapes are closed," Stone complains.

"I wish we knew which room was Drag's," you say.

"I don't know what good that would do. We can't see into any of them," says Lia.

"What's that noise?" asks Stone.

"Sounds like a cat meowing," answers Lia.

You move closer to the sound. "It's coming from inside that storage shed. Maybe it's Precious."

"Who's Precious?"

"Mrs. Stark's cat. I couldn't find her today, but I thought she was just hiding."

Stone shrugs. "Why would Drag steal a cat?"

"It's a blue Persian—worth a lot of money."

"That poor kitty. We have to get it out of the shed," says Lia.

Stone says, "No way. That door has a strong padlock. Let's go home."

"You can go," you reply. "It was my fault that poor Precious was catnapped. I can't just leave her."

Turn to page 139.

You think, *I wish Emily would help me. With all her brains, she might be able to figure out where the gems are hidden.*

You try to work out a plan as you get closer to the Norman house. You want Mr. Belden to think there are a bunch of people coming. Then he'll get scared and leave. You stomp up on the porch and holler, "Hey, Joe, help Susan with her luggage."

You make your voice sound deeper. "Sam's helping her. Do you have my rifle?"

The front door is unlocked, and you push it open, flipping on the hall light. "Come on, everybody, we'll . . ." Your voice freezes as you see the man in the doorway. He has bright red hair, and he grabs your upper arm in his big hand.

Choices: You kick his leg. He howls and lets you go. You turn and run (turn to page 87).

You stand there trying to think what to do next (turn to page 43).

You see your aunt at dinner. She says, "You flubbed your test, but I might be able to get you another part."

"I don't want a part. I get too scared."

"We're leaving at six tomorrow morning to go up to the Athabasca glacier. The planet Eyesig where our story takes place is covered with ice."

"I'd like to see the glacier, but you don't need to worry about getting me a part."

The next morning Aunt Marie says, "There's someone I want you to meet." She introduces you to a tall man.

He looks at you critically. "Sure, we'll use the kid." He nods at you. "Come on. Let's go to costuming."

"What do I have to do?" you ask.

"We'll tell you." He stops at a doorway and hollers. "I found another snow monster to replace the kid with strep."

A lady looks up. "Hurry, we don't have much time." She hands you a monster costume. It's covered with silver-green fur, and the hands have long, curved claws. It fits. She fastens the headpiece on. You feel as if you're suffocating. She adjusts it so you can breathe, but you can't see very well. She leads you to the door. "The bus is waiting," she says.

Choices: You pull off the mask. "I don't want to be a monster. I'm going home" (turn to page 44).

You walk to the bus (turn to page 10).

You trudge back and start at another block. Maybe you'll have more luck here. You ring the bell at a large brick home. "Would you like someone to take care of your house while you're on vacation?" you ask the lady who opens the door.

"I might."

You hand her the price list. She studies it, then says, "We're going to Yellowstone next week. I'd like the basic plan—plus pet care."

You write down her name—Mrs. Eldon Stark.

She explains, "We'll be gone two weeks. Come over Saturday to pick up the keys. I'll give you instructions on feeding Precious, my blue Persian."

You feel happy you have one customer. No one is home at the next two houses. You cross the street and see Drag Phelps tinkering with his old Ford. He's in high school, and he got in trouble for stealing a car last winter. You don't intend to talk to him, but he says, "Hey, whatcha selling?"

"Not selling anything."

"So how come you're walking up to all the houses?"

Choices: You tell (turn to page 20).

You say, "Don't have time to talk" (turn to page 22).

You find a shoe box and cut windows in it. You cover them with stiff plastic from a Christmas card box. Then you add beds cut from a piece of foam. Bits of fabric make sheets and blankets.

With strips of cardboard and tape you design chairs and a table. At lunchtime you set out lunch on foil plates for the family. The slivers of roast beef, pieces of raisins, and bits of potato chip will be a feast for them.

You take the family from the cupboard and gently lift each one into the new house. The children run around examining everything, but the mother and father talk together as if they don't understand what's going on.

You whisper, "From now on, I'm going to take care of you." You put the shoe box in your room. You make plans to add dividers to make more rooms in the house. This is more fun than you've ever had.

The next morning you notice they've moved some of the furniture against the wall. It looks as if they're trying to build a stairway to get out of their new house. You put the furniture back.

Choices: **You cut a door in the house (turn to page 104).**
You put the shoe box on the top shelf of your closet (turn to page 97).

You drop your sack of cherries and jump down from the tree. You run after Jeff. Your heart is pounding, and you can't seem to get enough air in your lungs.

The dogs' barking is getting louder, but you can't go any faster. You hear a man calling, "Stop! Stop, and I'll call the dogs off." But you don't want to get caught. You make your legs keep running even though your feet feel like lead weights.

You stumble as the lead dog dashes right in front of you. You cover your face as the snarling dogs snap and sniff at you. The old man cries, "Get the other boy."

The dogs go after Jeff. You sit up looking into the old man's piercing gray eyes. "What makes you think you can steal the cherries on private property?"

You stand up. "Somebody said you didn't want them."

"That somebody was wrong." He puts his hand on your shoulder and steers you toward the place where the dogs are barking at Jeff. Mr. Morton calls the dogs off. He takes his hand from your shoulder. "March to the house," he orders you and Jeff.

You march. There's no chance to run with the dogs there.

Mr. Morton calls Jeff's folks and your aunt and uncle. You feel terrible. You didn't think you were stealing, but you should have made sure Mr. Morton didn't mind. You've only been in Pineville one whole day, and already you're in trouble.

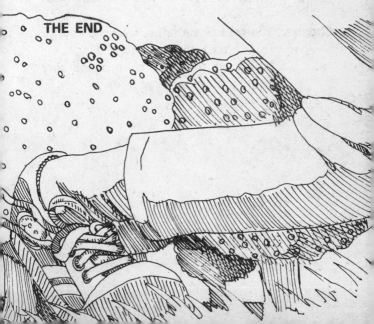

THE END

"No, but you don't want to breathe it. You better go to the park. Looks like a nice day."

But you're thinking, *If it'll kill cockroaches, it'll probably kill tiny people.* You shiver. "What time are they coming?"

"Nine." Grandfather grabs his briefcase, says good-bye, and hurries off to work. It's after eight, so there's not much time.

You lie on the floor in the kitchen and call into the hole by the baseboard. "Danger! The exterminators are coming. Please come out so I can help you."

You feel frustrated. Can they understand your words or does your voice sound like thunder in their delicate ears?

You finally stand up. You've tried your best.

Choices: **You take Grandfather's advice and go to the park (turn to page 35).**
You keep trying to contact the tiny people (turn to page 129).

Two days later you get up early and hurry to Grandfather's church to catch the bus to camp. All the other kids know each other, but no one pays any attention to you.

You notice a plump girl standing by herself. You wonder if she feels as lonely as you do. You walk over to her. "Ever been to Camp Greenwood before?" you ask.

"No, but I've seen pictures. There's a lake and lots of trees—like a forest. I've never seen a forest. Have you?"

"Ah, yeah—where I come from there are lots of forests."

"Where's that?"

"Seattle. It's way across the country—near the Pacific Ocean. Actually we're on Puget Sound, but that connects with the ocean."

"How come you're coming to camp here?"

"I'm spending the summer with my grandfather in New York."

Another kid asks, "Hey, you ever see Mount St. Helens?"

"Sure. It was a beautiful white cone before it blew its top. But a lava dome's growing in the crater so someday it'll look great again."

"Time to board," yells the youth minister.

You're looking forward to the cool lake and shady forest, but even more important are the friends you're making.

THE END

You hang up the phone hoping you've made the right decision. It would be fun to make a lot of money, but Aunt Marie doesn't seem happy. Sometimes she comes for a visit between jobs, but she's always worrying about whether she'll get a good part again.

Once she complained, "I can't go anywhere without fans recognizing me and asking for my autograph."

Later you heard Dad telling Mom, "She's more afraid of people forgetting her than mobbing her."

Mom added, "Poor Marie. When you think of yourself all the time, you miss a lot."

You think, *I've read about some of the child stars who never get to enjoy being a kid. I don't want to be like that.*

Choices: You decide to go to Pineville after all (turn to page 5).
You help Stone and Lia with their business (turn to page 14).

You pull your wallet out and buy a token. You shove the change from the five-dollar bill in your pocket. Dropping the token into the turnstile, you walk through.

The girl is still waiting on the platform, and you're glad you haven't lost her. Then the subway rumbles in and the doors open. You dodge exiting passengers and get on the same car as the girl.

The subway zooms through the dark tunnel under the city. The girl doesn't pay any attention to you. You're sure she doesn't realize she's being followed.

As the train rolls into one of the lighted stations, the girl gets off, and you follow her. She walks up the stairs and down a street. You stay a few steps behind. Soon you're walking between old brick apartment buildings. Some of the windows are broken, and there's garbage on the sidewalk.

A chill runs up your spine. You're afraid this is the part of the city Grandfather warned you about.

Choices: You turn and run (turn to page 122).
You keep following (turn to page 66).

Drag catches up with you and grabs your arm. "Let's see that bag."

You squirm, but Drag has beefy muscles and you can't get away. He throws out the milk carton and looks at the tape recorder. He grabs the bag, then knocks you to the cement. You gasp for air as he runs off with your recorder and the evidence.

You get up and walk back to the Alcotts. Your jaw hurts where Drag hit you, and your head aches where it hit the cement.

You find Stone. "What happened to you?" he asks.

You tell him the story.

"Better call the police," he says.

"I will. I don't want to take care of houses anymore. What if Mrs. Stark thinks I robbed her? I didn't know I'd have problems like this."

"But we need you."

"This is summer vacation. I'm going to have fun." You walk back to your yard and get your bike. You ride to the precinct station and report the incident with Drag. The police say they'll pick him up for questioning.

As you bike home, you think about what friends you could find to hang around with. But Stone and Lia are your best friends. You don't want them mad at you. You decide to keep working at house sitting. It wouldn't be fair to walk away just because you have a problem.

THE END

As you go by Alcotts you shout, "Stone! Lia! Somebody help me!" The twins are in the backyard, and they come flying out to see what's wrong. They run after you. Finally they catch up with you and help you pull Zacchaeus to a stop.

Zacchaeus howls, but you pet him and finally get him quiet. He starts licking the twins' faces. "That's Zacchaeus's idea of kissing. He really likes you," you explain.

"Why do they call him Zacchaeus? Does he climb trees?" asks Lia.

"Naw, Suzy Elliott named him that because that's her favorite Bible story."

"Goliath would have been a better name. He sure is huge," says Stone.

"I think he's forgotten his idea of finding his family, so I should be able to get him home." You walk Zacchaeus home.

You give him some dog food, but after he gulps it down, he starts looking for his family. You throw a stick, and he runs after it. You play with him awhile, then go to the Alcotts for lunch.

"What's that terrible noise?" asks Mrs. Alcott.

Turn to page 102.

"Wow, you're really good," calls Chris.

You wave and keep climbing. The spray of the falls is getting you wet, but you don't mind. When you get to the top, you look around. You call to Chris, "Hey, come on up. The view is great." But Chris has disappeared.

You'd like to do more exploring, but you decide you'd better get back to the car. You don't want to keep Chris and Mr. Dilmer waiting. You start down, but it's harder to see the handholds and toeholds looking down.

When you finally get to the bottom, you follow the canyon to the path where you came in. You walk through the woods until you realize you should have reached the car by now. Could you have taken the wrong path?

Choices: You retrace your steps (turn to page 107).

You keep going (turn to page 109).

You run until your side aches. Emily is right. Mr. Belden is mean, and you don't ever want to see him again. But then you think of Mrs. Fellar in the hospital. She should know what's going on.

The next morning you walk to the small hospital on Main Street. A nurse directs you to Mrs. Fellar's room. She's lying on her bed with a cast on her leg. She smiles at you.

You explain who you are and how you saw Mr. Belden at her house.

She sounds upset. "Oh, no! I thought he left town. I don't trust him. I think he left one of the stairs loose, hoping I'd fall. That's how I broke my leg. I must call my lawyer. Please get me a wheelchair."

You find a wheelchair in the hall and push it back to the room.

Turn to page 90.

You dash across the room as the woman reaches for her phone. You slip out the front door and run down the hall. You guess that the woman is calling the police, and you want to be far away when they arrive. But what if she remembers seeing you in the apartment house?

You go to a variety store and buy glasses and some stuff to make your hair black. You slip into a rest room. Looking in a mirror, you part your hair in the middle and rub the black stuff on it. You add the glasses and feel satisfied that the woman won't recognize you. You buy a navy T-shirt and put it on over your old one.

You walk back to the apartment. Two ladies are talking in the lobby. "Imagine a burglar breaking right through the wall."

"Nobody's safe anymore."

You ask, "What'd they take?"

"Nothing, but that was because Daisy dialed the police."

"I don't think it'll happen again," you say.

"How do you know?" demands the plump lady.

"Just a hunch." You leave before anyone can ask you any more questions.

THE END

A nurse rushes in. "What's going on?"

Mrs. Fellar explains, "I must make an important phone call."

"Doctor doesn't want you upset with your heart condition."

"I'll be more upset if I can't call my lawyer."

The nurse helps her into the wheelchair. "I can take her to the phone," you offer.

When Mrs. Fellar finishes talking on the phone, she says, "My lawyer will see that someone stays in the house until my son comes this weekend. He'll take care of everything. Thank you for warning me. When I get back to the house, you must come visit me. I'll show you the secret passage to the attic."

You grin. Mrs. Fellar is going to be fun to know.

THE END

You go back to your aunt's house. Emily is putting on her backpack. "Want to go on a hike?"

"Sounds good."

"Will you carry our lunches in your pack?" asks Emily.

"Sure. What're you carrying?"

"Just some jars."

You smile. There must be blackberries where you're going. You get your backpack and go to the kitchen. Aunt Joyce makes another tuna fish sandwich. When she finishes, she hands you two lunches, and you put them in your pack with some cans of apple juice.

You hike along the road after Emily. "Where are we going?"

"You'll see." She turns off the road on a trail leading upward.

Turn to page 100.

"Wait until you see where I'm taking you."
Emily sounds excited, and you suspect this is no
ordinary hike.

You don't like the feeling of not knowing
whether the land is going to hold you or drop
you into ooze. "Why are we walking here?" You
swat a mosquito on your arm.

"It's the only way to get to the pond. . . . There
it is."

You scowl. Emily brought you through that
miserable swamp to show you a pond covered
with brown scum. You were hoping to find
blackberries.

Emily kneels beside the creepy pond and takes
out jars from her pack. She scoops up some of
the scum. "What do you want that for?" you
demand.

"I'm studying diatoms. Fascinating one-cell algae." She picks up a rock from the water and two flat, colorless worms slide over its surface. "Planaria," she announces as she pushes the worms into a jar.

"Why do you want all this creepy stuff?"

She looks at you as if you're the weird one. "It's exciting to see all the life forms God made. I'm going to look at these things through my microscope." She scoops up more pond water.

"Can I look through your microscope?"

"Sure. You won't call this scum creepy when you've seen the patterns of the cells."

You think, *Maybe by the end of summer I'll be a brain like Emily. Won't Dad and Mom be surprised?*

THE END

94

That afternoon you put your tape recorder in a grocery bag. You cut a small hole in the bag so you can reach the buttons. You put an empty cracker box and a milk carton on top of the recorder. Then you pretend you're walking home from the store.

You stop as you see Drag's legs sticking out from under a car. "Hey, Drag, how about a cut of the loot?" You turn your recorder on.

He crawls out. "Whatcha talking about?"

"Stark place. I gave you the tip. Remember?"

"Maybe you did, but I took all the risks. I don't split with anybody. Get that straight."

"Don't get mad. Just thought I'd ask."

"Hey, you know anybody else going on vacation?"

"I might."

"Maybe we could work out a deal."

"You mean I give you the tips on who's gone and you rob the places?"

"Yeah, it really helps to know if people are gone for a while so you can take your time looking for valuable stuff." He grabs the cracker box. "Hey, this is empty. What's going on?"

You run.

Choices: You see a bus stopped at the corner, and you jump on (turn to page 71).
You run toward the Alcotts' house (turn to page 84).

You think, *What if that girl doesn't have any family? The Bible says we're supposed to love our enemies, but it's hard to love someone who cheated me.*

You say, "Grandfather, I keep thinking about that girl living in a burned-out building. I wish she could go to Bible camp."

Grandfather sighs. "I can talk to our youth minister. There are scholarships for poor kids. But don't go back in that neighborhood alone."

The next day the youth minister stops by to ask where the girl lives. You offer to take him there. His name is Steve, and you're glad he's tall and muscular.

Steve says, "If this girl doesn't have parents, I'll refer her to an agency who can find a foster home. Any young kid alone in New York is in a dangerous situation."

You find the girl who declares, "You can't prove nothing."

Steve says, "We didn't come to make trouble. Maybe we can help. Where are your folks?"

"They're a long ways away. I can take care of myself. I don't want anyone telling me what to do. Leave me alone."

You say, "Hey, don't get uptight. We're inviting you to summer camp."

Turn to page 96.

Steve adds, "You know—swimming in a lake, walking in the woods, that kind of action."

She scowls, "What's the catch?"

"It's a church camp. We're trying to help people find a new life by living on course with God who runs this universe."

"I don't have no money."

"It's free. We'll give you a scholarship," explains Steve.

She looks at you. "How come you're trying to help me when I sold you a free ticket?"

You say, "Jesus wants us to treat people like we want to be treated. If everybody did that, we'd all be happier."

"Won't work," she says.

"You'll learn more about how it works at camp," says Steve.

She wrinkles her nose. "I'll go. I'd go anywhere to get out of this heat."

You smile. You're going to pray she'll become a Christian.

THE END

You think, "Even if they get out of the box, they'll never get down from that high shelf. They should be glad I made them such a fancy house. I'm going to take them home with me. Man, but all my friends will freak out when they see my family of little people."

You have a sudden inspiration. "I bet everyone would like to see my tiny people." You pick up the box and head for a television station.

You walk in the door and speak to the receptionist. "Would somebody here be interested in tiny people no bigger than a pin?"

She frowns. "Everybody's very busy right now."

You set the box on her desk and lift off the lid. She peers inside then screams, "Rod, come here! You're not going to believe what this kid has."

That afternoon they bump a garden expert off a talk show and put you on—coast to coast. You tell how you found the tiny people as the camera zeros in on the people and the house you made. Unfortunately the tiny people are petrified, and they all cower in a corner. You lift the father up and set him on a table. He tries to get back to the rest of the family.

"This is no trick," says the host. "These little people are really alive."

Turn to page 105.

You go back to your room and start memorizing your lines.

The king is your father, but Crugo, the evil prime minister, has kidnapped you and sold you to the snow monsters. They live on the surface of Eyesig. Your father's kingdom is a series of large underground caves. Your aunt is also a slave, and together you plan how to return to your father and defeat the treacherous Crugo.

You study all day. The next day you begin rehearsals, and life becomes really hectic. Acting is hard work, and the director yells at you a lot. Aunt Marie says you'll get used to it, but you're not sure you ever will.

In a couple weeks, you move to Hollywood to do the underground scenes. Aunt Marie takes you around to meet several big stars. You meet Lance Arman who stars in "Golden Galaxy," your favorite TV show. He says, "I remember when I started. It was a lot of work, but anything worthwhile is work."

"Yeah, you're right." You wish you could think of something more original to say, but you can hardly believe you're standing here talking to Lance Arman.

A photographer walks by and stops. "Let me get a picture of you and the kid." Lance puts his hand on your shoulder, and you both smile. Man, the kids at home are going to be impressed with that!

Turn to page 101.

"How far are we going?" You're sweaty from the hot sun.

"Not too much farther," she says.

But it seems far. Finally the trail leads down through evergreens to a lake. You flop down on a grassy mound.

"Let's eat lunch," you suggest. Emily agrees. The sandwiches taste good after all that hiking. After you eat, Emily leads the way around the green lake and then heads across a grassy area.

Your foot sinks down into thick mud. "Hey— this is a swamp," you complain.

Choices: You say, "I'm going back" (turn to
page 54).
You follow Emily (turn to page 92).

After the pilot show is finished, you and Aunt Marie take a tour of several cities to advertise it. You appear on talk shows, and the hosts keep asking you how it feels to be a star. You tell them it's fantastic fun.

You call Stone and Lia to tell them to watch you on a talk show. But they don't talk very long. They're getting ready to go to a beach party. You feel a pang of loneliness as you think of your friends. You're going to dinner at a fancy restaurant, and you have to dress up. Aunt Marie says it's important to impress the right people. It would feel good to relax once in a while.

When you return to Hollywood after the tour, you begin to get requests for your picture and autograph. You sign your name on a bunch of pictures. Aunt Marie's secretary takes care of mailing them. But you read all the letters. The kids rave about your looks and personality. If your name wasn't on the letter, you'd think they were writing about somebody else.

Then comes the big news. The network will make the show a regular series.

You try to decide what to do. Do you want to grow up in one big leap with a full-time job? Doing one film was a great experience, but a series could tie up your life for years.

Choices: You agree to stay in the cast (turn to page 30).

You say you want to go home (turn to page 127).

You explain, "Elliotts' dog doesn't like to be alone."

You go back to Elliotts after lunch. Mrs. Beecher, who's on the crabby side, comes to her back fence. "You'll have to keep that dog from howling. My husband is not well, and he can't stand that noise."

You take Zacchaeus to your backyard. It's fenced, and you hope he'll stay quiet while you lie on the chaise lounge and read a science fiction book.

But soon a neighbor's black cat comes strolling through the yard. Zacchaeus runs after the cat, barking like crazy. The cat jumps on top of your folks' greenhouse. Zacchaeus tries to reach the cat and goes crashing through the fiberglass. The cat escapes, Zacchaeus howls, and you pull the dog away from the mess. You snap his leash on and fasten it to the fence.

"Bad dog," you scold. "You've probably ruined Mom and Dad's collection of rare South American plants."

Zacchaeus hangs his head as if he's sorry. You pat him. "That's OK, Zack. I'll fix the greenhouse." It'll take all the money you've earned and then some, but you have to save your folks' plants.

THE END

The Metropolitan Museum is huge. You like the Egyptian stuff. They even have an Egyptian temple built in a big room. Wow!

Your favorite room is the one with suits of armor. You wish they'd let you try the armor on. You wonder how it felt to clank around wearing hunks of metal.

You recall studying God's armor in Sunday school last year. You try to remember all the parts to fight life's battles. There's the helmet of salvation. You have that because you've asked Jesus to forgive your sins and lead your life. The shield of faith is to stop the temptation arrows Satan aims at you.

The sword is the Bible—that's your weapon against the enemy. The breastplate is goodness. Sometimes your breastplate gets holes in it. You're glad God forgives you when you do something wrong.

Your invisible armor is better than this heavy stuff—as long as you remember to use it.

THE END

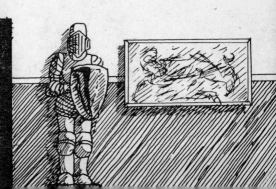

The next day when you wake up, the family is gone. You leave the shoe box near the baseboard all day, hoping they'll come back, but they never do.

That evening Grandfather steps on the box as he's fixing dinner. "You'll have to move your play stuff out of the kitchen where I'm working," he says.

"Sure." You take the squashed box back to your room and dump it in the wastebasket.

Your secret adventure is over, but you'll never forget the little people. You're glad you saved them from being gassed even though no one else will ever know about it.

THE END

The next day a man who introduces himself as Professor Dawson comes to the apartment. He has a device to magnify the little people's voices.

He holds the tiny microphone down to the father. "Please, let us go free. We have not done anything wrong. Why are you keeping us in prison?"

You speak through another device the professor shows you. "How can you call the house I made you a prison? You have plenty to eat. Now that we can talk, you can have whatever you want."

"We want our freedom. We'd rather die fighting cockroaches than be stared at like we're freaks."

"Hey, I saved you from being gassed. You should be glad for all I've done for you."

The professor says to you, "I've been authorized to offer you a hundred thousand dollars for these people. I'll provide them with a comfortable environment. I want to study them."

Choices: **You take the money (turn to page 119).**
You refuse the money (turn to page 144).

You bring Mr. Fisher the price list, and he tells you what he wants done.

"I'll take good care of your place," you promise, feeling sad to notice how slow he moves.

"I just had my ninetieth birthday so I don't move as fast as I once did," he explains.

"Ninety years! That's a long time."

"No, it's not long. It goes by very fast. But Jesus promised me eternal life, and that's never going to end. I've been studying an atlas of the stars. I'm figuring on exploring the universe with my new resurrected body."

"How do you know you can do that?"

"I don't know for sure, but you remember after Jesus arose, he could appear wherever he wanted, and then he went up to heaven. I figure I'll be able to move like that, too. First thing I'm going to do when I get to heaven is say thank you to Jesus, then I'm going to ask where the Galactic Travel Agency is."

You laugh even though you're swallowing a lump in your throat. "Be sure you don't land in any black holes."

THE END

You go back to the canyon, but you don't see any other trail. You're puzzled. Then you notice a strange thing. A small cedar seedling has fallen over. You look more carefully. It looks as if some seedling trees were hastily planted to block the trail. That's why you missed it. Someone deliberately tried to hide the trail.

The Dilmers! They were trying to make you get lost, and you played right into their hands by climbing the rock wall. You're furious, and you rush back to the empty parking lot. You follow a short road to the highway.

Cars speed by. You can't remember which direction Banff is.

**Choices: You walk to the left (turn to page 31).
You walk to the right (turn to page 120).**

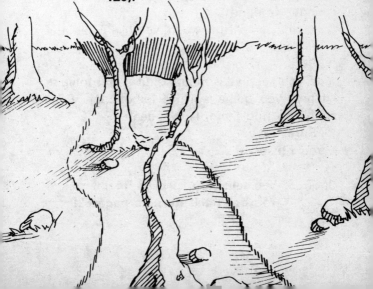

You say, "I better get home, or my aunt and uncle will start looking for me. They know I came here to investigate a light."

"I don't believe you. Keep working."

"My cousin Emily is watching the house with her telescope. When I don't come back, she'll call the sheriff."

"The brain's your cousin?" His voice has a worried tone.

"Yeah. Your red hair showed real clear in her telescope. I think you better let me go before you get in trouble for kidnapping."

"I didn't take you no place."

"You made me come down here, and you're forcing me to stay."

"Now, look, kid, I gave you a job. You don't want the job, you can leave."

You climb the ladder quickly, hoping he won't change his mind.

He whispers, "How would you like a fistful of valuable gems?"

"Sure."

"If you keep your mouth shut about tonight, I'll give you gems worth a lot of money—as soon as I find them. Is it a deal?"

"Sure."

You run home.

Choices: You tell (turn to page 141).
You don't tell (turn to page 63).

You trudge onward. This path may lead to a road. But then you notice you're beginning to climb. What if the path leads up the mountain?

The mosquitoes are huge, and your face begins to itch, from their bites. You scratch and big welts rise on your face. The repellent you put on earlier must have been washed off by the spray from the falls.

A cold sensation settles in your stomach. You wonder if Chris and Mr. Dilmer deliberately left you in this mosquito-infested area so you'd look too bad for filming.

It's getting dark. You find a large, partly hollow tree stump. You tear off evergreen branches and stack them next to it. Then you curl up in the hollow stump and pile branches on like a blanket. You worry about freezing in the night. You imagine hikers stumbling over your stiff body, and tears run down your cheeks.

Before it gets light, you're up stomping around, trying to get your chilled blood circulating again. As soon as it's light enough to see, you start down the trail. Your mosquito bites itch like crazy.

When you reach the canyon, you see two hikers. "Which way is the parking lot?" you call.

They point to the trail, and you follow it to the lot. A park ranger is getting out of a car. You tell him your story, and he drives you to Banff.

Turn to page 114.

Emily grins. "I think my burglar bomb is a big success."

"It'll sure surprise the burglars," you agree.

You go home with Emily and pretend to go to bed, but as soon as she's in her room, you sneak back to the Norman house. You're going to find those gems, and you don't plan to tell anyone.

You hurry to the basement. Ignoring the smell, you shake every pear can you can find. They all slosh as if they have pears in them. You feel really disappointed. Finally you see one more pear can in a corner behind some corn. It doesn't make any noise when you shake it.

Every nerve tingles with excitement. You rush up to the kitchen. You open the can with a can opener. Packed in cotton are big, sparkling gems! You're rich!

Then you hear Mr. Belden's voice. "Hand over that can, kid."

Turn to page 112.

You turn to see his muscular figure. He's holding a knife in his right hand.

You give him the can. He smiles at you, showing crooked, discolored teeth. "Don't know how you found them, but it sure saves me a lot of trouble."

He orders you to the basement and down the ladder to the root cellar. He puts the wooden trap door down, and you hear him lock it. You're stuck in this awful, moldy, pitch black hole.

You hope that eventually somebody will find you. But how will you explain that you lost the gems? . . . If you're still alive to try.

THE END

You rush down the hall after him. He still has the little girl in his mouth. He runs down the stairs and out the front door just as someone comes in. He crawls into a hole under the stairs, but you can't follow him. The hole is too small.

"Here, kitty, kitty," you plead.

Then you see a pushcart on the sidewalk. You run to it. "I want a wiener—no bun."

"No bun?" The man looks at you as if you're strange. "Mustard?"

"Just the wiener. Hurry!" You hand him the money.

As you rush away with the wiener, he calls, "Come back when you get another wiener attack."

You kneel by the hole. "Here, kitty." You hold the warm wiener close to the hole.

The cat grabs the wiener with his teeth. But where is the girl?

You reach your hand into the dirty hole. You feel a small human shape. You pick her up in your cupped hand. She's not moving. You blink your tears away and rush back upstairs. You gently place the lifeless girl in the pan with the rest of the family.

The mother cradles the girl in her arms. She hugs her mother. She's alive! She must have fainted from fear. You're happy enough to turn a cartwheel, but not on the fire escape. You carry the pan back to the apartment.

Turn to page 126.

When you walk into the hotel lobby, you see the director striding across the rug. He stares at you. "What happened to your face?"

"Mosquitoes."

"You look terrible. We have to start filming today. Do you know your lines?"

"Not yet. I've been lost. I didn't mean to be gone so long."

The director scowls at you. "I can't use a lumpy-faced kid who doesn't even know his script."

"I learn fast, and we can cover the bites with makeup."

"No makeup will hide those lumps."

As if on cue, Chris appears. "I know the lines, Mr. Austin."

He looks at Chris thoughtfully. You cry, "It's not fair. It's Chris's fault that I got lost."

Mr. Austin shrugs. "If Chris knows the lines, that settles it. Sorry. You can be a snow monster. No one will ever see your face."

But you're thinking how those bites will itch under that monster headpiece.

THE END

Your heart's beating at a furious rate. You don't think you could run if your life depended on it. You hope the dogs are so busy chasing Jeff that they won't notice you flattened against the gnarled trunk.

You close your eyes and wish you could wake up someplace else.

The dogs are barking like crazy now. You peek around the trunk. They have Jeff surrounded. They're jumping on him. Then you see the old man limping toward them. He calls the dogs off and marches Jeff back to his house.

You say to yourself, "I'm sorry I let Jeff talk me into stealing Mr. Morton's cherries."

Choices: You wish there were some way to help Mr. Morton (turn to page 132).
You decide it's time for a cherry feast (turn to page 6).

"Hi, Emily," you say.

"Oh, hello. I need some help."

You try to take shallow breaths to keep from breathing more than necessary of the foul-smelling air.

Emily hands you a test tube. "Keep shaking this. I don't want the chemicals to separate."

"What are you making"

"A burglar bomb. If a burglar enters a house, my bomb will let off a terrible gas smell that will drive him away quick."

"How does the bomb know it's a burglar?"

"I haven't figured that out yet."

Turn to page 18.

You stop digging and say, "If Mr. Norman was old and sick, he wouldn't have had the strength to dig in this hard dirt."

"What do you know about Mr. Norman?" barks Mr. Belden.

"I know he hid his collection of gems. But you're looking for them in the wrong place." You start to climb the ladder.

He mutters, "I've looked everywhere. He kept them in the library safe, but sometime when I was gone, he moved them."

"Maybe he buried them outside."

"No, he never even got dressed those last few weeks. He could still walk, but he spent most of his time in bed. I took care of that cranky old man that last year. I deserve the gems."

"Wonder why he didn't tell his daughter where they were," you say.

"Phone wasn't working. I cut the line soon as I realized he had hid the gems. They belong to me, and I'm going to find them." His brown eyes look wild and strange. He grabs your arm. "If you help me find them, I'll split them with you. We'll both be rich."

"I'll try to think of places to look. I better get home now before someone misses me." You edge past him toward the basement stairs.

You run home. You hope you don't see Mr. Belden again. He's weird!

Turn to page 118.
Turn to page 118.

The next day Aunt Joyce asks, "Will you go over to the Norman house and water the plants? Susan asked Emily to water them while she's away, but Emily went to the library this morning, and she may stay there all day."

"Sure, I'll go," you say.

She hands you the keys, and you run up the hill road to the Norman house. You want to look for the gems yourself. If you find them, you won't have to split with Mr. Belden.

You hurriedly water the plants. Then you start looking for the gems. You walk into the living room and look for loose bricks in the fireplace. You go upstairs into a big bedroom. Someone has been searching here. The dresser drawers have all been removed. Maybe Mr. Belden thought he'd find a secret compartment.

You look around, trying to think where Mr. Norman might have hidden his gems. You pick up the Bible on the nightstand. As you open it, you see a paper with writing: Matthew 6-19-6, Psalm 89-6-6, Luke 2-24-19.

That's strange, you think. *Usually Bible verses are marked by two numbers—chapter and verse. What does the third number mean?*

Choices: You put the paper in your pocket (turn to page 123).

You put the paper back in the Bible (turn to page 136).

As he hands you a check, you think of all the things you can buy—almost anything you want. The professor takes the little people away. You hope they'll be happy. All day you keep thinking about the father's words: "We want our freedom." You know you wouldn't like to live in a box with giants staring at you.

THE END

You walk along the road looking for a gas station or store.

Finally you see a car stopped ahead, and you run toward it, hoping the people will give you a ride to Banff. Two gray-haired ladies are staring at a flat tire. "What are you going to do now, Ethel?"

"I don't know, Phyllis." Ethel sees you. "Can you tell us how far it is to a service station?"

"No, I'm looking for one so I can use the phone."

Phyllis says, "I wish you were a man so you could change a tire."

"I've watched my dad change tires. Do you have a jack?"

Ethel opens the trunk. "We'll have to take our suitcases out."

Phyllis shrugs. "If you think you and a child can change a tire, you're crazier than I thought."

Ethel retorts, "At least we're doing something more than wringing our hands." Ethel takes out the suitcases, and you take out the jack and the spare. Jacking up the car is a lot harder than it looks when Dad does it. But between you, you get the car up.

Phyllis says, "If that jack slips, you're going to get hurt."

"The jack won't slip." Ethel tries to remove the lug nuts.

Finally the spare has replaced the flat, and Ethel's dirty face wears a triumphant look. They drive you to Banff, arguing all the way. They stop in front of your hotel. "Thanks for the ride," you say.

"Thanks for your help," says Ethel.

Turn to page 135.

122

Before you get to the end of the block, three tough guys block your path. "This is a toll sidewalk, and we're the toll collectors," says the tallest one.

"Don't have any money." Your heart is beating like a jackhammer.

"You'd better have five dollars, or we'll make you work it off."

"Doing what?"

"Cleaning our headquarters."

You pull out your wallet and take out a five-dollar bill.

The tall guy grabs the bill and your wallet. "Hey, there's thirty bucks here."

"Give that back." You try to sound tough, but you feel like a rabbit confronting a bunch of lions.

"Cool it. You can walk on this sidewalk any time. Not many kids get to do that." He flips the empty wallet back to you, and they step aside.

You run as fast as you can, hoping you won't run into any more tough guys. Your side aches, and you stop. Then you see a mass of trees and you hurry toward them. It's Central Park.

Choices: When you come to the Metropolitan Museum, you go inside (turn to page 103).
You keep walking until you get back to the apartment (turn to page 65).

That evening you look up the Bible verses. You wonder if the third number means the word in the verse. Maybe Mr. Norman was trying to leave a message for his daughter where he knew Mr. Belden would never look.

Matthew 6:19-6—"Lay not up for yourselves TREASURES upon earth."

Psalm 89:6-6—"For who in the heaven CAN be compared unto the Lord?"

Luke 2:24-19—"And to offer a sacrifice according to that which is said in the law of the Lord, a PAIR of turtledoves."

TREASURES CAN PAIR. You scowl. That doesn't make sense. What comes in pairs? Shoes, socks, bookends. But those things all must have been searched. You feel disappointed. If Mr. Norman was trying to leave a message, he sure wasn't making it clear.

That night after you go to bed, the words keep going through your mind. TREASURES CAN PAIR. What if *can* is a noun—not a verb? You remember all the cans of food you saw in the basement. What if Mr. Norman used PAIR to make it more difficult, but he really meant *pear?* You feel excited.

Choices: You go to the house (turn to page 145).

You decide to wait until daylight (turn to page 124).

You wake up in the middle of the night hearing loud sirens. You jump out of bed and hurry to your window. Oh, wow! The Norman house is on fire. Flames leap from the windows. Firemen rush around with their big hoses.

Your aunt and uncle are standing in the yard with coats over their nightclothes. You put on a raincoat and join them.

Aunt Joyce is crying. "Poor Susan. She wanted to fix up that house to live in. Now look at it."

Uncle Pete adds, "Doesn't look as if there'll be much left. I wonder what started the fire."

You keep watching until the fire is out. A blackened corner is still standing, but the house is a total loss. You hear later that the firemen think vandals broke in and did a lot of damage. Then they set the fire.

You think it must have been Mr. Belden, but nobody knows what happened to him. You wish you had told your aunt and uncle about seeing him. Maybe they would have known how to stop him. You'll never know if he found the gems. You like stories that have an ending. It's terrible not knowing who set the fire or what happened to all those gems.

THE END

You put the pan down and run after the cat. You look in all the halls, in the basement, and then outside the building. But you can't find the cat. He's disappeared with the small girl.

Wearily you return to the apartment.

The man has his arm around his wife as if to comfort her.

"I can't find the cat," you say in a choked voice. "I'm sorry. I didn't know there were cats around. I shouldn't have left you. I just didn't think about the dangers." You hope they can understand, but you're afraid your loud words are only frightening them more.

Turn to page 126.

The apartment doesn't smell anymore, so it's safe for the little people to go back to their home. You put the pan by the kitchen baseboard and lift each person out. They march single file into the crack in the wall.

"Good luck," you whisper. "With the cock-roaches gone, life should be a lot better."

You never see the tiny people after that. But every evening you leave a small square of foil with food saved from your dinner. By morning the foil and food are always gone.

THE END

It feels great to get home and see Stone and Lia and your folks, who have returned from Brazil.

Stone says, "I saw you on TV."

Lia adds, "All the kids in school are really excited about knowing a TV star."

"How long will you be here?" asks Stone.

"This is where I live—remember?"

"You're not moving to Hollywood?"

You shake your head. "It was fun to make the film, but I don't want to decide on a career yet. I want to have kid fun. I don't like being around a bunch of people who call me *dahling*, when most of them would stab me in the back if they thought it would get them a good part."

"But isn't it fun to have people asking for your picture and your autograph?" asks Lia.

"Sure, it's fun. But I don't want to get like some of the actors whose only aim in life is getting star parts and making money. Maybe someday I'll go back, but not now."

THE END

You try not to think about what the Starks will say when they come home and find their house robbed. You grab your swimsuit and walk over to Fullers with Lia and Stone.

He's taking care of the Fuller house. Mrs. Fuller told him he could use the pool. "Sure would like a pool like this," you say.

"Yeah, I want to be rich," agrees Stone.

Lia says, "Rich people aren't always happy."

"Maybe not, but I'd like to try it. Hey, I just got a fantastic idea."

You're wary of Stone's ideas.

He goes on. "Why don't we charge admission to the pool? We could make a bundle of money."

"I don't think Fullers would like that," you say.

"They said we could use it. If we charge a dollar a kid, we can make money faster than walking dogs and taking in mail. The kids around here really need a pool in this hot weather."

Choices: You shake your head. "It wouldn't be right. Count me out" (turn to page 57).

You say, "Let's try it for a day and see how it works" (turn to page 32).

You call, "Danger, danger! All cockroaches are to be killed by a spray. Please come out, or you'll be gassed, too."

But no tiny people appear. If only you could shrink to their size, you could lead them to safety. But that's impossible.

All that hollering made you thirsty. You go to the refrigerator for orange juice. You don't see any, but there's a bottle of apple juice. You pour a glass and take a big swallow.

Yuck! It wasn't apple juice. You feel dizzy. You sit down and close your eyes. You're scared. The bottle must have contained one of Grandfather's chemicals. You remember he warned you not to eat or drink anything unless it was labeled.

You open your eyes and look at the blue sky. No, that's not the sky. You're in a gigantic room with a blue ceiling. As you look around, you realize what's happened. You're as small as they tiny people. Your clothes—and even your watch—have shrunk.

Turn to page 130.

Eight fifty-five! No time to waste. You bend down and slip into the tiny hole between sections of the baseboard. The light is dim, and you feel your way along the narrow tunnel. Huge chunks of dirt keep hitting your face. You realize they'd be bits of dust to a regular-size person. You put up your hands to shield your face.

In your new soft voice you call, "Please, come out. I can help you escape from the poison gas." You don't see anyone, and with your short legs, you can't move very fast. You hear a noise and turn around. A huge black cockroach with an open mouth is coming closer and closer.

Choices: You duck into a small, dark hole (turn to page 21).

You run as fast as you can (turn to page 38).

You laugh. "I don't have the part yet. The director may not like me."

Lia passes the cookies. "I think you'll get the part, but we'll sure miss you."

Stone adds, "If they need any more kids, we're available."

"I'll write and let you know how things go."

Stone says, "With all the money you'll be making, you can call us. I'd sure like to be a rich star."

"I'm not even a small asteroid yet," you point out. "Don't count on me being a star."

Turn to page 37.

When you get home, you ask Emily, "Do you know Mr. Morton?"

"Why are you asking?"

"This kid talked me into picking cherries at Mr. Morton's place. He said nobody wanted them, but that wasn't true."

"Poor Mr. Morton. He loves that cherry orchard too much to sell it, but he's too old to manage it any longer. Maybe there's a way we could help him. Our youth director tells us we should live our faith—not just talk about it. I'm going to call him and tell him about Mr. Morton."

The next morning you and a bunch of kids from Emily's church head to Mr. Morton's orchard to pick cherries. Mr. Morton sets up his roadside stand, and he sells cherries while you pick. The rest of the cherries will go to the cannery. He says, "I can't believe you kids are working just to help me."

Dean, the youth director, smiles. "Christ gives us a lot of joy when we help others."

While you're picking, you all sing choruses. Some of the people buying cherries stop to listen.

When you're taking your lunch break, the dogs come around wanting to be petted. Even they know things are a lot different today than they were yesterday.

THE END

134

The next morning you walk over to Jeff's house. He says, "You bring anything to put the cherries in?"

"I thought the place supplied you with flats."

"We're picking for ourselves, and we're going to sell the cherries. We'll make a lot of money that way."

"Does your dad have a cherry orchard?" you ask.

"Naw. The orchard belongs to old man Morton. He's too old to pick, so the cherries will go to waste if we don't pick them."

"Are you sure he doesn't care?"

"He won't even know we're there."

"Maybe we should ask him if it's okay?"

Jeff snorts. "What'sa matter? You scared?"

"No, I just want to know what the deal is."

Choices: You add, "I just remembered something I need to do. Can't help you today" (turn to page 91).

You follow Jeff to the orchard (turn to page 61).

It feels good to get back to the hotel. Chris and Mr. Dilmer come in a few minutes later. Chris explains, "We came back here to get help and organized a search party, but we couldn't find any sign of you."

"You couldn't have looked very hard. Why didn't you wait for me? I got to the parking lot eventually."

"Hey, we walked up the trail and you weren't there."

"I got on the wrong trail because you blocked the right trail."

Aunt Marie says to you, "Everything turned out fine, so let's not argue anymore. We're like a family. Let's go to our rooms, and I'll order you some dinner. Tomorrow's a big day—your first day of filming."

You nod. You have a long script to learn before tomorrow. You know you'll never trust Chris again. You silently pray, "Thank you, Lord, for bringing me back safely. Don't ever let me want a part so bad that I'd hurt someone to get it."

THE END

You keep looking in Mr. Norman's room. You even search the papers in the wastebasket. Stuck on the bottom is a small paper with the letters *WYWERBPSSO*. It must be a code! Mr. Norman left a message for his daughter. You rush home to find Emily to see if her computer can decode the message in a hurry. You meet her carrying a load of books, and you tell her about the paper.

She says, "If the code letters are in sequence, my decoder program will figure it out. If Mr. Norman made a complicated code, it'll take longer."

"I don't think he'd make it too hard for his daughter to figure out."

Emily hooks up the computer and types a bunch of instructions. "All I have to do is type in the letter that stands for *A*, and the computer will instantly figure out the rest." She keeps changing the key letter until the message on the screen says *SUSANXLOOK.* "That's it," she cries. "*E* stands for *A*, *W* stands for *S*, and so on."

"But that doesn't tell me anything." Disappointment washes over you.

"Looks as if Mr. Norman gave up on the idea of leaving Mrs. Fellar a message, or maybe he was too sick to continue." Emily looks at you. "Don't feel so sad. Why don't you write another coded message and see if my computer can decode it?"

You nod. You might as well forget Mr. Norman's gems. "Maybe I can get a computer," you say hopefully. "Then we could write letters in code and have our computers figure them out for us."

THE END

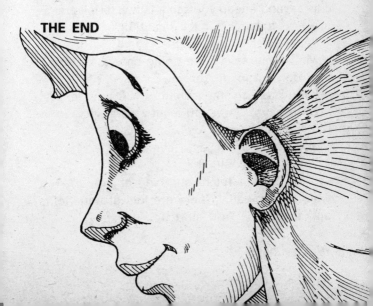

You go with Chris and Mr. Dilmer as they drive to a canyon. "Beautiful spot," says Mr. Dilmer. "The waterfall is spectacular."

"Sure is nice of you to take me along."

Chris grins. "We're friends."

After Chris's dad parks, you start walking through the forest path.

Mr. Dilmer works as a cameraman. He says, "Chris is going to be a big star one of these days—when the right part comes along."

You feel uncomfortable thinking how you got the part Chris wanted, but you're glad to have a friend. Mr. Dilmer has a bottle of insect repellent, and you all splash it on to discourage the dive-bombing mosquitoes.

Finally you walk into the rock-walled canyon where a stream passes over rapids. The canyon curves, and ahead you see a tall waterfall crashing into a pool. "That's beautiful."

"Fantastic," agrees Chris.

Mr. Dilmer says, "I'm going back to the car."

"I don't want to go yet," says Chris.

"You kids can stay awhile." Mr. Dilmer leaves.

Chris says, "I bet you'd get a great view from the top of the rock wall."

You study it. "I could climb it."

"I bet you couldn't."

"I've done a lot of climbing at home." You walk to the wall. "There are lots of handholds and toeholds." You start up.

Turn to page 86.

You try to think of a plan to rescue Precious. Then you hear voices, and you crouch behind some bushes. You hear Drag say, "Got some good stuff—TV, silverware, diamond rings. Know where I can sell a pedigreed cat?"

You peek between the shrubs. An older man says, "You out of your mind? A cat's too hard to handle."

"Guess I'll hold it for ransom then."

"You'll get caught and blow the whole operation. I'm giving you orders, Drag. Kill that cat quicklike."

You shudder. Poor Precious. You run back to your house and call the police. You gasp your story, ending with "Hurry before they kill Precious."

"Who's going to get killed?"

"Just hurry!" You hang up and rush back to Drag's. The police arrive while Drag and the man are loading a truck. The police handcuff both Drag and his fence.

"Where's Precious?" demands a policeman.

"Don't know what you're talking about," answers Drag.

Turn to page 140.

You slip into the shed and pick up Precious in her box.

"Who are you?" calls a policeman.

"I'm the one who called. I'm taking care of Precious."

The policeman laughs. "A cat! We thought Precious was a girl. That's why we rushed here so fast."

The other officer adds, "It's a good thing we did. We've just solved a lot of burglaries."

You take Precious home for a good meal of salmon cat food.

THE END

You wake your uncle and aunt and tell them what happened.

Aunt Joyce calls the sheriff and tells him Mr. Belden is hunting for the gems while Susan Fellar's in the hospital. When Aunt Joyce hangs up the phone, she says, "The sheriff's getting a court order to prevent Mr. Belden from going to that house. He'll be arrested if he's caught there."

"But what if Mr. Belden finds the gems before the sheriff can get the court order and stop him from looking?" you ask.

"Mr. Norman hid them very well. It's going to take someone more clever than Mr. Belden to find them."

You nod. "He doesn't act very smart." You're glad you had a part in helping Mrs. Fellar.

THE END

Stone looks disgusted.

You don't want Stone mad at you. Finally you think of another idea. "Why don't we put a notice on the church bulletin board?"

Stone says, "We can't take places that are too far away."

"Let's figure out the area we want to work, and we'll put that down."

You write the notice that afternoon and take it to the church. You meet Pastor Newman, and you tell him what you're doing.

"I'm always glad to see young people with ambition," he says. "I'll put up your notice."

The next week you get several calls from church members, and you arrange to take care of their houses. One is an elderly friend of your father's who doesn't have much money. He's going to visit his daughter.

Choices: **You feel you shouldn't charge him (turn to page 143).**
You charge him the same as everyone else (turn to page 106).

You remember how he used to whittle wooden toys for you when you were small—tops, boats, and even little people.

You go to his house. "Mr. Fisher, I'll take care of your place. Just tell me what you want done."

"I'd like you to feed the fish in my aquarium. I've left instructions. I'll give you my key. Can you close the drapes every evening and turn on some lights so it'll look as if someone's home?"

"Sure, I'll do that."

"You'll have to come over in the morning to turn off the lights and open the drapes."

"That's fine."

"How much will this cost?"

"It's free."

"But I thought you'd started a business."

"You're my friend. I'm glad I can help you."

You say good-bye and walk home. You'll have to put some of your own money into the computer fund, but you don't mind. It feels good to help Mr. Fisher.

THE END

You take the box to the kitchen baseboard and slowly turn it on its side. The father leads his family back to their hidden room in the wall.

Professor Dawson calls, "What are you doing?"

"I'm giving them their freedom. That's what they want."

"Stop! Stop!" he shouts as he rushes to the kitchen.

"They're gone," you say.

"You fool! We might have learned great scientific truths from studying them."

"But they're people even if they're small. If I took money for them it would be like slavery. I should have known how they felt. I wish I had never taken them to the TV studio. If I had it to do over, I wouldn't tell anyone about them."

THE END

You pick up the key to the Norman front door and slip outside. It's windy, and you shiver as you hear the wind rustling the tree branches. But you're more afraid of Mr. Belden and his wild eyes than you are of creepy noises.

You're close to the house when you hear a car coming up the driveway. Your heart pounds as you duck behind a bush.

Mr. Belden gets out of the car. He pulls an ax and a crowbar from his trunk and heads for the house.

You figure he's going to chop up the house looking for the gems. What are you going to do?

Choices: **You hurry home to call the sheriff (turn to page 60).**

You run back and wake Emily (turn to page 56).

Aunt Marie says, "I've arranged for you to attend drama school."

"But, won't that spoil the natural talent everyone's talking about?"

"Look, if you want to go to the top, you have to work at it. We start filming episodes in a month, so you don't have much time."

"Can't I at least go to Disneyland?" you ask.

"Oh, sure, we'll schedule that. I think you have a Saturday free next month. We have to keep promoting the show, remember."

You think, "Being a star isn't as much fun as most people think."

THE END

You and Emily go in the house turning on lights. You leave the front door wide open to air it out. "Ick! It smells like a gas leak," you say.

"Why don't we come back in the morning," suggests Emily.

"Mr. Belden may be back before then. We have to find the treasure and keep Mr. Belden from doing any more damage." You lead the way down the stairs. The smell isn't as bad in the basement.

Emily follows muttering. "Nobody's been able to find those gems."

"I know where they are. Quick, help me shake the pear cans," you order.

Emily looks at you as if your rocket has slipped out of orbit.

"The gems are in one of these cans," you explain. "Yell if you find one that doesn't slosh." As you're shaking cans, you tell Emily about the biblical clues.

She says, "All the ones I've picked up slosh." But a minute later she calls, "Hey, here's one that doesn't have any juice."

You rip off the label and see a soldered patch.

You and Emily rush back to home and open the can. It's filled with beautiful gems!

Emily jumps up and down. "Mrs. Fellar will be thrilled to get her gems." Then she says, "You're a real brain to figure out those clues."

Imagine Emily calling you a brain!

THE END

"I got trapped between the boards because I was tiny, but then I started growing bigger and I couldn't breathe. I didn't mean to break your wall."

The woman scrambles against the headboard of her bed. Her eyes reflect fear. The curlers in her hair are bobbing as if she's shaking. She reaches for the telephone.

You say, "Don't be scared. I won't hurt you. Somebody'll fix your wall. The building must be insured."

Finally she speaks. "You poor child. I'll call someone to help you. You just sit down."

"I don't need any help. Hey, I'm not crazy. Really, I'm not." You decide you better leave quick before someone comes to lock you up. No one will believe how you got trapped between the walls.

THE END

Zacchaeus keeps running as if he's in a race, and you hang onto the leash. You try to figure out how to stop him.

As you come to the highway, you see a station wagon just like the Elliotts'. Zacchaeus gives a happy bark and charges after it. You let go of the leash. You're not brave enough to dodge speeding cars.

Zacchaeus disappears, and you run back to the Alcotts'. Lia is sitting on the front porch. "Where's your mom?" you call.

"She's at church getting ready for the potluck."

"I need a car. Zacchaeus is running down the highway."

"Why'd you let him get loose?"

"He's too strong for me. What am I going to do?"

"Pray that some dog lover picks him up before he gets killed."

You feel sick. Poor Zacchaeus. You wish you knew how to find him.

That night when you and the Alcotts return from church, you stop on the porch and listen. "That's Zacchaeus," you cry.

You rush over to the Elliotts' and open the gate to let the dog in. He stops howling and gulps down a bowl of dog food. You wait for him to fall asleep, but every time you start to leave, he opens his eyes and howls.

You take him back to the Alcotts'. He jumps on your bed, so you sleep on the floor. You resign yourself to having a shaggy companion wherever you go the next two weeks. You hope the neighborhood appreciates the price you're paying for their peace.

THE END

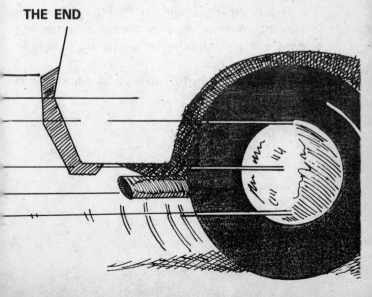

You watch the house from your window. You see the light in the basement, but you can't see what's happening. Finally you go to the telephone and call the sheriff. "There's somebody in the Norman house," you explain.

"Who is this?" asks a curt voice.

"Just a neighbor. There shouldn't be anyone in that house when Mrs. Fellar is in the hospital. It might be Mr. Belden trying to find Mr. Norman's hidden gems."

"Thanks for your report. We'll investigate if we have time."

"Okay, thanks." But you have a feeling that the fellow you talked to wasn't much interested in a kid's report. You should have had your uncle call. He might have listened to a grown-up.

That night you dream you find the jewels. You bite into a hamburger and crunch something hard. It's a diamond! The jewels are hidden in your hamburger.

What a letdown to wake up and find it was only a dream.

THE END